Frank G

FRANK & AVA
Unrequited Love

outskirtspress
DENVER, COLORADO

This is a work of fiction. The events and characters described herein are imaginary and are not intended to refer to specific places or living persons. The opinions expressed in this manuscript are solely the opinions of the author and do not represent the opinions or thoughts of the publisher. The author has represented and warranted full ownership and/or legal right to publish all the materials in this book.

Frank & Ava
Unrequited Love
All Rights Reserved.
Copyright © 2012 Frank Gariboldi
v2.0

Cover Photo © 2012 JupiterImages Corporation. All rights reserved - used with permission.

This book may not be reproduced, transmitted, or stored in whole or in part by any means, including graphic, electronic, or mechanical without the express written consent of the publisher except in the case of brief quotations embodied in critical articles and reviews.

Outskirts Press, Inc.
http://www.outskirtspress.com

ISBN: 978-1-4327-9364-7

Outskirts Press and the "OP" logo are trademarks belonging to Outskirts Press, Inc.

PRINTED IN THE UNITED STATES OF AMERICA

Foreword

I am not sure Why does one write a book?

Yet I knew I had to write this one from the first day I heard, "In the Wee Small Hours of the Morning." Frank Sinatra had died about two weeks ago, and there were still some articles being written about him and his life, and I remember reading one by Pete Hamill, and Pete recommending the reader to listen to the "Wee Small Hours." Well, I went out and purchased the CD, and I was "hooked."

I was born on December 15, 1931, a 16-year-and-3-day separation from Frank's birth date, but still a December child. We were both married in Our Lady of Sorrows Church at 24 years of age in different cities. Both our parents came from Italy with mothers less than 5 feet tall and dominant in the family. We were both "only" children and weighed over 13½ pounds at birth and had difficult births. We both had problems with our left ear, were Pavarotti lovers, prolific readers, drank Jack Daniels, did not sleep well, had lots of energy, and most important, we both had a "Don't tell me what to do!" attitude. And last of all, we both had a fascination with sweaters.

Maybe those are the reasons that I had to write the book. Whatever the reason, the story in my head had to come out.

I grew up in the late '40s and early '50s, and Frank was never one of my favorite singers. My father's love of opera possessed me first. I went to see *La Traviata* before I saw Joe DiMaggio play ball. First came Nelson Eddy and Jeanette

McDonald, then others followed. In my teens, my friends and I followed the Battle of the Baritones and one of my favorites was Tony Bennett. Tony stayed in my life for a very long time until he was pushed out by Pavarotti, Springsteen, and Bocelli, and then taken over completely by Frank.

Have you ever been taken over by something? There is not much you can do. Go with the flow. Nurture the dream. Stay with the dream. Enjoy the rush, the enthusiasm, and the warm glow.

Well, Frank wrapped me up, and I am still enraptured by his music, and I feel with every fiber of my body that Ava wrapped him up and changed his life and voice from their first encounter.

Yes, this is a story that grew inside of me that had to be written. At first, I read many books and articles about Frank and his life, so this book has some facts and some truth. The story has as much truth as any life lived, as much truth as can be pulled out of the life of Frank Sinatra. I looked at some short subjects on Frank, his mannerisms, the way he spoke and acted. I even looked at a few of his movies, just to try to get the feel of the man. Getting to know the man from this distance is not easy, when even those close to him may never have known him.

Some of his life I have lived. An only child, my father always working, a strong willed mother who would give her life for me, and by the way, so would my father. I grew up alone on the streets of New York City and Corona, NY. As a young boy of 6 I had a near-death experience about which my parents knew nothing, and I never thought or understood about until my early forties.

My first wife, Dottie, who died at the age of 54, had brought in a palm reader to the house and had invited girlfriends over to have their palms read. I had gone out for the evening with the boys and upon arriving home found out the reader was still there and I was persuaded by Dottie to have my palms read. A rather strange and yet unexplainable moment took place. This woman, whom I had never met, looked at my palm and exclaimed to me that I had been given a second chance. I had to think for a while, and then I remembered at the age of 6 having a "terrible" earache on my left side, and then recollecting the experience of leaving my body looking down at myself in the bed and walking above the bed toward a hooded figure with a staff who was directing me to the living-room window which had turned into an opening. As I entered this opening I awoke. My temperature that had been hovering around 105 to 106 broke. The pus or whatever was in my ear ran out onto the pillow. And my mother who had been sent to the church to pray by our atheist doctor because "he had done all that he could do" came running up the stairs with my father yelling out to her "Pierina, Pierina, he is okay, he is okay." (In their Italian dialect, of course.) As I grew older I always thought my mother must have really bargained with God, "He's my only child, you have to save him. I'll tell you what I will do . . ."

This experience sent me away every summer to get "fresh air" (doctor's orders) until I was 14. For 8 years I traveled up to Goshen, NY, to stay with the Salesian brothers. Those years were fun and also very lonely.

In those early years I was alone quite a bit, and I always felt that since I was always being sent away, I had to take care of myself, that no one was there for me. I had dreams of grandeur but never a dream like Frank's, his one and only dream of being a premier singer.

I am what you would call a "late bloomer." And I owe my new life to God, who made that all possible.

When I got to know Frank Sinatra I was already in my 60s, and he really captured me. In the music and the books that I heard and read came the thought that Ava could have been the real reason that Frank began to sing the way he did. That Ava was the reason for his "bel canto."

The story started to take place almost immediately as I began to jot down notes and write some story lines. This took a few years to put together, and then finally in 2007, I decided to write my book. I was 75 years old and writing about Frank who was also 75 years of age in my story.

I prayed a lot and many mornings I began with nothing and after prayers five pages would roll out of my head down to my fingers and on to the computer screen. With Lorraine, my wife, leading me on, being my editor and director in this process, the book began to take shape.

This book is part fiction, part truth, and as my grandson Joey said to me, "Papa, it's a historical novel." Now that sounds impressive.

Well, that is what this book is then, a historical novel made up in my mind. My thoughts, my words, a story conceived by me as to how Frank could become the premier singer that he did become. The words became a love story about his voice, his love of music, and those people who shaped the voice.

In my own way I think Frank would have appreciated the story. I think he would have toasted me, as Italians have done for hundreds of years, with drink in hand and said *"C'in, c'in."*

Acknowledgments

I want to thank my wife Lorraine for always being there for me. She lovingly called me her "author" as I arose early in the mornings to begin my writings. She was my editor. But primarily, she was always there leading me on, encouraging me, showing me and telling me in many ways that I could write and tell my story.

I also want to thank Kevin and Maryjane McQuade for their expertise in English, correcting and adding punctuation marks and giving me small hints to make the words and phrases more understandable.

My grandson Joseph Leo, III, has also become part of my Sinatra story. He has assisted in putting the music together so I could pick the songs out for the "show" in my story. He has also made me stretch my imagination in making many story lines into more artistic forms. He has helped me add more to the Sinatra–Gardner mystique, and I thank him for that.

In the words of Frank Sinatra,
   "... some people get their kicks stompin' on a dream ..."

Chapter One
Beginnings

Frank came into the room—this was His Room. He was probably the only person in the house who truly loved this room. Barbara came in once in a while, and the servants came in to clean and tidy up, but this was His Room. The room itself was not a large room as some of the others in the house, but was the right space that he needed to think, to internalize, and to be himself. This room, as far as he was concerned, was the only room in the whole house that mattered.

This was His Room!

He had designed and coordinated all that went into the room so that only this room would express his special likes. The curtains, over the large windows that overlooked the spectacular garden and pool, were clear and bright, so that the sun could come in and give that special look that only sunlight can give to a room.

The chairs, couches, lamps, tables, and other accessories that made up the room were all handmade especially for him.

The color orange was splashed everywhere. Not too much orange, but you knew that the color orange meant something to this man.

THIS WAS HIS ROOM!!!

"What kind of shit did I pull last night?" he said angrily. He was annoyed at himself, pacing the floor from the large window near his desk which faced the pool, a desk that was clear of everything except some writing paper and a cup filled with cigarettes and another filled with white mints. A few pencils were splayed across the top of the desk, almost like Pick Up Sticks.

Frank was angry with himself. Last night at the Universal Amphitheatre, he was a disaster. Fumbled lines, missed cues, unable to see the teleprompter. This all added up to a terrible show. He was a disaster on stage. He had even tripped, not once but twice, over his own feet. Can you imagine that? What had happened? He was ready to rage against the stage crew, but when he looked down, there was nothing there, only his own two feet and a bare floor. Even his voice had failed him. Trying to reach the high notes was a strain, and one time he just stopped. He knew he could not touch that note.

"What the hell's goin' on? I know I'm 75, but that doesn't mean I'm fallin' apart. This is the second time I've pulled this crap in the last 3 months. Is this how Alzheimer's starts? Now that's scary shit!" he mumbled to himself as he stopped and let that thought roll around his head.

"No! No! No!" he shouted. "What the hell's happnin' to me? I'm Frank Sinatra, and I can't let that happen to me, and I won't let that happen to me!!!"

This was the man who had sung before presidents and heads of state. This was the man who had probably touched more lives with his singing than any other personality in the world. This was the man who had staged presidential inaugurations. He had sung in just about every country in the world, in front of millions of people, and had sold millions of records, albums, and CDs, and whose movie and singing career spanned over 50 years. This was Frank Sinatra!!

As he paced the floor, he reached for a cigarette in one of the special glass containers that were placed around the room just for him and his friends' convenience.

"No! No! No!" he blurted, and pulled away from the cigarettes as if he had just touched a steam pipe. "I gotta be ready for tonight's performance. I'm not gonna let that happen again. This has gotta stop. Just my tea and no cigarettes. Shit! I've done that before. Nothin' until showtime. These people come to see me and hear me sing."

As he said this he sat down in the padded chair behind his desk, picked up a white mint, uncovered the cellophane wrap, placed the mint in his mouth, then folded his arms across his chest and began to breathe slowly, thinking of these people, millions of them, who had made him who he was.

Frank had always been loyal, sometimes to a fault. If you were his friend there was nothing that he would not do for you or buy for you. His generosity was legendary. Buying cars for friends, throwing parties of lavish proportions, loaning money out and sometimes never getting paid back, paying for hospital bills for those friends who could not afford to pay them. His worldwide benefits made millions of dollars for the beneficiaries of these events. In most cases, he not only gave of his talents, but paid all the expenses of the event, the musicians, the plane fares, everything. He was quite generous.

Yet, if you became his enemy, look out. And many times you became his enemy through no fault of your own. He dictated that. He was the one who cut you off and cut you out of his life. The break could be words said in the wrong context, a look given at the wrong time, a rumor gone haywire.

Sometimes words and sometimes action set him off and cut you out of his life.

He controlled your friendship. His way was the only way. And this was not due to the fact that he was one of the biggest stars of Hollywood or the world. This was not because he was a friend of presidents or heads of state. This was because his life was to be his way, and he had been doing this life his way for the last 50 years.

As he slouched back in the chair, a frown on his face, arms still crossed, he began to think out loud. "What the hell's goin' on? I didn't drink that much before the show. Shit, I was just at the doctors a few weeks ago, and he said everything's okay, maybe except for my lungs. But I still can hit the high ones, and I can still hold on to the long ones. The voice is a little rough around the edges, but I can't let go, and they won't let me."

The "they" he was referring to were the fans that came to see him over these last 50 years. From the beginning there were the bobby-soxers who had made him a star and continued this love affair as they got older. When the guys came back from the war, they began to come to his shows, go to his movies, buy his records, now his CDs, and watch his TV shows. "They" were really the fans, the reason he performed, the reason he lived.

He needed them as much as they needed him.

Artie Shaw had once said that he got out of the business because he could not take the show, the people, the travel, but "Frank Sinatra, he could not live without it."

This was certainly true; Frank could not live without his fans.

Frank loved to record his songs. He enjoyed making movies; they made him the superstar that he had become. But, being on stage, singing, talking, and making love to the audience, his audience, in the only way he knew how and the only way that he could, was really his life. The singing, the stage were his lifeblood. That and only that was his love, his first love, and he cherished, nurtured, protected, and took care of that love as a mother would her child.

Singing in front of an audience filled him with the love that he probably was not sure he was getting from the people that surrounded him most of the time. The audience, those fans, they were what the singing was all about for him. They did not talk back; they only gave him applause and adulation. They did not fight him, there were no arguments, no one was trying to vie for his attention, and no one wanted his money. He never could cut them out of his life. They belonged to each other.

Only there on stage could he truly be himself. Only there on stage could he really project himself and be vulnerable. This was the place where he showed emotion and pain. This was where he took the lyrics and the music and blended them into who he was. Oh yes, in the recording studios he did a terrific job. But on stage he was vulnerable; one song, one take, that's all he had. He was wide open for the world to see. He had to admit to himself that years ago he really did sing with more emotion, but there were some songs that still resonated with him and he was able to bring back all the feelings and emotions that the composer and lyricist had put into their music. The stage was home for him, and the audience was his first and primary love.

The audience was first; they may even have come before his family. He was not sure about that. But there on the stage in front of them was where he could be himself, where he felt needed, where he felt wanted. He needed their affirmation that he was somebody. All the awards in the world never told him that. Only these people shouting loud and clear that they loved him and they never let him down.

All they wanted was for him to sing, to make love to them with that special voice that he had. And the cracking or raspy tones did not make any difference to them. So what if the voice was not in the best condition? You see, they also felt like he did. They loved him. This was a mutual admiration, going back 50 years. And for those 50 years, with an exception of a couple of years in the early fifties, they loved each other.

Artie Shaw was right. Frank needed them, those people who paid their hard-earned dollars just to see him, and they, in turn, needed him. He could not live without them.

Frank relaxed a little as he began to think of these people who had paid to hear him sing last night and who have been there for him all these years. He knew how they felt about him. He could feel that as soon as he came on stage. He always gave his best to them, and last night, he had betrayed them, and even with that, they still applauded him and made him feel like a million bucks. They weren't concerned that his voice cracked a little or that he even tripped or even got lost on the words. They wanted to see him, to visit with him, to know that he was still there for them, just like he had been there for the last 50 years. He was a part of their life, and he could do no wrong as far as they were concerned. You see, he was family and sometimes in a family people goof up and you still love them. You let go of those little faults.

As one guy said when being interviewed after last night's disaster, "It's okay; he's allowed an off night; and we know that the voice is not like it used to be, but he is still better than most of the guys singin' today. He puts them all to shame; I'd rather spend my money on Sinatra than payin' half to listen to anybody else. He still turns us on. He's Sinatra, and that's all that matters to me and my wife."

Frank knew this as he shifted in the chair and placed his arms on the desk, resting his head on top of his hands as he gently began to think of these people who have been with him for over 50 years.

"Man, I remember the Paramount as if it was yesterday. The guys weren't there, but the girls, my God, the broads, they were everywhere. Bobby-soxers, that's what they called 'em. Yellin', screamin', swoonin'. That fuckin' George, what a great job he did with the girls payin' some of dem a few bucks, and it worked like a charm. That George was a good man. He did all right for me.

"That was some openin'. The curtain opens, I walk out, the girls scream so loud that I get chills right down to the bottom of my toes, and Benny says, 'What the fuck was that?' What an openin'!!! I'll never forget dat.

"I never had so many broads after me in all my life. Shit, when I walked out of the Paramount in dose days, dey had to have police guards surround me and dose bitches still got to me. Rippin' my jacket, grabbin' my balls and my ass. Some of dem were real mean. I remember one day they almost choked me to death. One of dem grabbed the end of my bow tie and another one grabbed the other end, with me in the middle, and they wouldn't let go. I saw stars; my eyes were poppin' out. Thank God for the cops. They clobbered the arms of those two broads. Man, they were chokin' me out. Stupid, fuckin' broads."

Frank frowned while thinking about this incident and many others. He then smiled because there were other times that he could have his pick of any one of them and those were enjoyable moments.

Frank began to relax a bit. He sat back in the chair, folded his arms across his chest, left the present, and went back in life. to some place in his mind where such things are stored to be picked out and reviewed at different times. This was such a time for Frank.

"Man, my parents really didn't want me to sing, especially my mother. She wanted me to be some kind of engineer. Shit I couldn't even add 2 and 2." A broad smile came across his face, the same smile that continues to thrill audiences all over the world.

The combination of that smile, those blue eyes, and his voice—what a gift to the world.

"And when I quit that cement job, they literally threw me out of the house. My father said, 'If you can't work, get out and find your own way. You can't stay here.' Just like that and he was gone.

"I tried that for a while, livin' in the city, tryin' to make ends meet. Nancy even gave me some money for music lessons. What the hell was his name? Quinlan or Quinon? He was good. I didn't go a long time, but he taught me about holdin' notes. I even used to go the 'Y' and swim, just to hold my breath underwater. And Quinny was always on my back to listen to the opera singers and classical music. Even to listen to the instruments. He would always say, 'Your voice is like an instrument. You have to control your voice, regulate, raise, or lower it, up or down. Treat your voice gently. Stop smokin'. That's no good for the voice.' Shit the only time I ever stop smokin' is sometimes before a show, like right now."

Chapter Two

Music Lessons

That thought brought him back to the present as he scowled and muttered, "Damn last night! What the hell was wrong with me? That shit has gotta stop. I gotta see what's in these pills the doctor keeps givin' me and Barbara keeps askin' me if I took my pills. I should throw this crap away."

Now he was sitting up, looking around the room for the pills. If he had found them they were certainly going to be thrown out. He then remembered they were up in his bedroom, and he was not about to go up there just to throw pills out. "I'll get them out later," he blurted out loud, and then looked around as if someone was watching him.

"They got me talkin' to myself. I gotta throw those things out."

As he settled back, his mind immediately went back to the memory studio in his head. "John, John Quinlan, that's his name. I remember when I first met him, and he heard me sing. He almost threw me out of his studio. 'You call that singing?' he screamed at me. 'What kind of a chicken voice is that? I am an opera voice teacher. I don't go in for that stupid stuff they call music. Are you sure you came to the right place?' Man, was he pissed. I had to plead with the guy. In fact, I had to beg him. Nancy had given me his name she got from a friend. I think that may have been the first and last time that I had to do dat, beg. All I could do is plead with him that this was my whole life. This is all that I ever wanted to do. I was cryin' and beggin' at the same time. He kept turnin' me down. Well, my persistence finally got to him. He agreed to see me for a few lessons, this one and the next one, and then he would make a decision. Quinny made that clear from the beginning. He was the boss, and I had better listen or I would be out on my ass. That son of a bitch charged me for that half hour and never gave me a lesson. I started to argue, but he took me by the arm and said if I did not like the rules, get out and do not come back.

"He was good, but beside not havin' the money for him, shit, I didn't have money for anything. Nancy paid for a few of the lessons, and then some. It was a good thing that Nancy was working. She was really a good kid. She loved the hell out of me," he reminisced.

"After a few visits I guess he could see the passion that I had for singin', even though the music wasn't his kind of music, and he began to take me more seriously.

"He taught me some good stuff, hold the note, keep the voice pure. 'You have a good voice, good range, but you're rather soft like a guitar. Learn to use the microphone. Read the lyrics. Get to know those lyrics like they were yours. Like the writer wrote those words just for you and you have to tell the audience what he told you. The words have to become yours; then, and only then, will that song have any meaning to you or to the people who are listening. Listen to opera! Listen to classical music! Pick up the music of Puccini or Brahms. Listen to Puccini's arias sung by Caruso or Gigli, how they hold the note, how each syllable is pronounced, how each word melts into the other giving each word its own feeling, its own meaning. Feel the music. You have to understand the words to get the feeling, and all the great opera singers know that.' John told me this could be done to my music. 'When Brahms put his chords together, each one blending with the other, you can feel the excitement, the joy, even the tragedy. Listen to them; they can teach you more than I can give you.'

"Hell, I wasn't a classical guy, but shit, opera was always around me growin' up. All the Italians that I knew would play opera on the radio or on their phonographs if they had one. We had one of dose, and I even convinced the old lady to buy some opera by Puccini, and I listened and learned. That Puccini was quite a ladies' man and smoke? He must've smoked a ton! They have a statue of him somewhere in Italy, and he has a cigarette in his hand. Can you imagine? He must've outsmoked Smokey."

As he said this, he paused in his thought process as he remembered his good friend Sammy Davis Jr.

"John taught me a lot, but I was a good student. I wanted to be the best. I wanted to be the next Bing Crosby. Man, he had style.

"I also learned a lot from Tommy. When Tommy played that trombone and took that extra breath, silently, quietly, and holding on to that note, my God, that was heaven, pure heaven. That's what I was able to do. That's what I taught myself. Swimmin', runnin', controllin' my breath.

"And the lyrics. I pronounced that fuckin' word over and over again until that became part of me, until I could feel the lyrics in my bones, until I could feel the sound in my soul. Shit, that was another world, another time.

"When nobody was home I would play that phonograph and listen to the opera by Puccini and the music of Brahms.

They really became part of me, especially Puccini. I couldn't get enough of him.

"I remember bein' up in my room, alone, no radio, just me and my song sheets. And at that time, I really didn't connect opera with the songs I was singin'. But, back in my room at night, that's where I started to put all the stuff that John taught me all together.

"I probably didn't know, but I was startin' to put my own style of music together. I'd go over the lesson John had drummed into me that day. I would think about my voice, soft, not much punch, but if I learned to use the microphone and learned how to speak and pronounce the words properly, I knew I could do it. My style was different, but Crosby was always in my head, and John, that son of a bitch, was constantly, constantly surroundin' me, and I could hear him repeat over and over, 'It's your lyrics; you're the singer, you're the one that they listen to. Make it your song; do not copy anybody else. These people come to hear you, not the songwriter.'

"Make it yours. It's sad; sing it that way. If it's happy, make them smile. Tell them a story, make them listen, make them cry, make them smile, make them listen to you and never forget you. Remember, the lyrics are a story about someone and most likely someone out there who needs to hear the words, who needs to suffer with you or to be happy with you. You have to sing so you touch their heart and souls. Don't just put one word on top of the other; put feeling into the music, interpret the lyrics, read the story and come at that song from all the angles you can think of. Then pick the one that you think the lyricist was thinking as he put the words down on paper and let that song becomes yours. 'Yours! Yours! Yours!' he would scream at me. 'You have got to find a way to touch their souls. Remember, once you open your mouth, the music and words become yours. The musician and lyricist give the song a body, but remember, remember, you, and you alone, give it a soul. You're the one that brings life to the song.'

"Music is a mystery. The notes have a way of raising your spirit, and in some ways, they can bring you down. Magic, that's what the notes are, magic, and only those who can feel the music, who have the ability, who have the soul for the music, can convey that magic to others. They can make their audience cry or smile. They are the ones who can make hearts flutter. If you want to be just a singer, then get out of here. Those are a dime a dozen. But if you want to be one of the great ones, then learn, study, and practice.

"Make your voice into an art form. Anybody can sing a song. But to raise the music with your voice into art . . . Now you're going somewhere. Now when you do that you separate yourself from the rest of the other singers. They will be just singers while you become the maestro. You will leave them in the dust.

"You! You! You will be the one that they will want to hear. You will be the one to bring bel canto into pop music.

"You can do it! Listen to me and learn.

"Work the lyrics until they become part of you, until the three of you—the music, the lyrics, and the voice—are one and the same, and then that song begins a life that will beat in the hearts of all the people that are listening to you.

"'Don't ever forget this. You are in control! You are in control! Your song, your song!' Man, he was a bitch on wheels, but he was good; he was good."

Frank paused in this reverie as he thought back on those days and the words of John. He smiled gently and nodded in silent agreement to the memory of John Quinlan.

"I began to read the lyrics word for word, pronouncin' the word like they wrote it. Not like I speak with the guys or the rest of the world. It was like a new language. I would immerse myself into those lyrics, each word being pronounced clearly and distinctly and softly.

"I remember using a dictionary so I could understand the word, and then try to interpret what the lyricist was trying to convey. That dictionary and Quinlan's book became part of me for the rest of my life. I still go to the dictionary when I'm stumped on a word that somebody has spoken to me. I was giving myself an education. I couldn't speak worth a shit, but when it came to a song, well, that was another language, and I learned it all at night, and all the time in my room and sometimes on many nights I would be under the covers with a flashlight reading and pronouncing words. What an education!

"Shit, I had to be quiet or the old man or the old lady would come up and knock the crap out of me. Especially the old lady. She always came home late, and if she heard me she would come in and scream and slap me around. She was quite the woman.

"I guess I take after her. I'm not like my father. He took a lotta shit from her. I asked him about that once, how come he never says nothin' and he lets her go on and on, and in his own quiet way he told me, 'Frank, I just listen, take it in, and I don't say nothin'. For me that's okay.' I guess for him that was okay. Although I don't know that I was any better around her. I never knew when she was gonna slap me or kiss me. She always had to be the center attraction. When she came in a room, she took over. It became her room. I do that when I sing. When I sing, it becomes my room."

Frank became quiet as his mind went from room to room where he had sung. From the beginnings at the Rustic Cabin, then the rooms with Harry James, the rooms with Tommy Dorsey, and then to all the rooms all over the world.

Then he fondly remembered Rio de Janeiro, El Estadio De Maracana, an open amphitheatre. That was the night 175,000 people showed up in the rain to hear him sing, at the time the largest audience ever to see a performer. They were going to cancel. Rain had been predicted, and the weatherman did not disappoint them. Rain all day but heavy stuff, sometimes—real ugly. People started showing up several hours before the show started. Two hours before showtime the place was about half-filled and the people were still coming in. Frank made a decision that he could not disappoint this audience. The show would go on. Everything was done to cover electrical wiring and to ensure that no one would be electrocuted. The stage was not too bad and was fairly well covered to protect the performer from the rain, yet the audience, that audience that kept filling up the seats, they would be unprotected and the water never stopped coming. There were umbrellas everywhere. Even Frank could not get over their enthusiasm to come and listen to him sing.

As he was getting ready to go onstage, the rain subsided, clouds began to disappear, and the sun appeared. No more water! No more rain!

Frank sang for 1½ hours, and then sang three more songs as an encore. He rarely did encores. But "this room" and this audience had mesmerized him. The audience went wild. Frank was always in awe of his audience, and even as he thought about that moment, he could feel the goose bumps all over his body.

That was some night! And do you know that the moment he walked off the stage, the rain started in again just as hard as earlier in the day.

Now that was a room he would never forget.

Making people cry and laugh and feel good about themselves. Seeing the eyes of his audience. He always did that. He had that special knack of making them think that he was only singing for them, that one individual. You could almost hear them say, "He's singin' to me, just me." The music, the lyrics became one. John Quinlan had taught him well, and he had learned well, and he had that innate talent to be able to put the lessons together and make them work to perfection. His phrasing, his timing, his inflection, his control, showed a spirit, a spirit of life in all the sadness and in all the joy. He became "The Voice."

"How long have I been doin' this? Fifty, 60 years? I'm a lucky son of a bitch. This is all I ever wanted to do. Sing! And I've been at it for a long time. Even before the Rustic Cabin. I guess I started as a kid when I sang at parties and stuff like that. The folks couldn't keep me away from singin'. I know they tried, but I knew what I wanted and stuck to it. That's a good thing. I couldn't do anything else. Can you imagine me a cement hog or a fireman like my old man? Never! Never!" he shouted emphatically.

"When I entered that Major Bowes contest and won, I knew that I was gonna be a singer and the best around. I wanted to be the best around, just like Crosby was at that time. Boy, did I envy him. In the movies, singin' with all those broads. Well, I didn't do too bad. Not bad for a high school dropout."

Frank sat back and thought about those beginning years. There they were almost like they happened yesterday. School was never his thing; he did not like studying, yet the lack of education was something that he missed dearly, not the schooling but the learning. He sometimes did not like the way he spoke, like one of the boys, one of the street guys. He would sometimes be angry at himself when he was in the company of friends and think back to the days when he could have been better educated.

He did read a lot, almost a book a week. He especially loved biographies, Washington, Lincoln, both Roosevelts, Booker T. Washington, Garibaldi, Columbus, da Vinci, Mussolini, and Machiavelli. And he always kept up with the local and national news. And for many years he carried a dictionary around with him. A kind of a self-education. He could speak to anyone about most topics, and if he didn't know a topic, he would look for those books on that topic and inform himself of that subject. He never wanted anyone to make a fool of him. Frank had a lot of pride.

As he pondered all these things, he arose and went to the opposite side of the room. There on the wall were many of his awards. In a very prominent position, although not in the center of that wall, was his academy award for Maggio in *From Here to Eternity*.

"Man, that was a real boost in the ass!" he exclaimed out loud as his mind traveled back to those days when nothing was going right and the newspaper guys were ready to dump him and look for the new "Sinatra."

He had only been singing professionally for about a dozen years. Disaster was about to strike him down, and suddenly out of nowhere, Maggio comes along and saves the day.

"Where the hell is that book? I know it's here; I only looked at it a couple of weeks ago. I told them never to move that damn book because I still go to it from time to time. It's my bible."

This book was in a special place of honor among the hundreds of books that lined the wall of his room. He reached down, and his hand automatically closed in on the book.

He picked up his treasure, *The Elements of Style* by William Strunk Jr.

"Man this book is old," he said very quietly. This was his "bible"; a book that he had purchased after Quinlan's recommendation.

"He told me to buy this book and read the book from cover to cover as many times as possible. Pronounce all the words. Memorize its strategies. 'It's all in the words, it's all in the words,' he would scream at me. That first book fell apart in my hands. This has gotta be another edition."

As he looked at the book more closely, he saw "third edition" on the top cover and E. B. White was the editor.

"This little book certainly taught me a lot about my lyrics. How to pronounce them, each word specifically, because I've only got 2 to 3 minutes to convey a message and each word has a meaning and each word connected to the next has a message for me to convey. That's how I saw this book. That's how I read it.

"Look at this on page 21, item 16. 'Use definite, specific, concrete language.' That's what the lyricist does when he puts words to the music. He only has a few minutes to deliver his message. He has to be very definite and specific and concrete in the words he uses, and when I sing those words, I have to convey that message.

"Too many singers just pick up the song sheet and sing. Hell, you can't do that. You gotta read the words, study them, ya hav'ta go into the head of that writer and feel the music, and then you have to be the interpreter of that song. It's the only thing that has any meaning to me. It's my interpretation of the music and lyrics written by another guy.

"The music, the lyrics, I'm the interpreter of all that. I have to glide over into a note or above the note, to pronounce every syllable of a word and connect to the next so that the words have meaning and feeling. It's the only way to sing. Like the violinist Heifetz, when he lets his bow glide over those strings, hits the high Cs, and then races down to hit the low ones, and yet, when you listen to him, they all come together there, all put together in a special way. He plays with feeling; it's smooth, like silk, puttin' everything of himself into that piece of music, and when he is finished, you know that you have heard the best, that you have been honored to be able to listen and feel that wonderful music.

"That's how I always wanted my music to sound. I always wanted my voice to be like that instrument, to put my heart and soul into a song so that when the audience listened, they could understand every word, could place themselves into the song, feel what I feel—moody, happy, sensual, excited, loving, depressed. Whatever mood that song conveys is what I want to convey when I sing. I was lucky to have such great composers and lyricists when I started, guys like Cole Porter, Irving

Berlin, George Gershwin, Jerome Kern, Rogers, and Hart. They wrote the love songs, and I was there to be able to sing all their songs. What a lucky bum I was.

"I used to practice a lot more, take the time to review each song, get the feel for the lyrics. I haven't been doin' that lately. Maybe that's why I was such a jerk last night. Not enough practice! Not enough time!

"'Be short, be brief, and avoid needless words.' That's what this guy Strunk says in this book. 'Avoid needless words, avoid needless words, and avoid needless words.' That's what Strunk says. And that's what the lyricist has to do when he puts the words to the music. He only has a few minutes to say something with any kind of meaning. He has to avoid those words that don't mean anything and get to the message.

"I guess that's where I learned to do only one take in the movies and even with the songs. I had gone over the words, the lyrics, again and again in my head that I knew exactly what I had to do or knew what I had to sing, although I did do more takes with my singing than with my acting.

"Everyone thought I learned the one take from Boris Karloff. He only affirmed me. Nah! It was Billy! Billy Strunk Jr.

"Too bad I never met Billy Strunk Jr. Him and I, we could have a lot to talk about. I owe him."

As he slowly riffled through the book stopping at one page or another, he smiled as some memories crossed his mind. He really spoke another language when he was in that room reviewing the lyrics, studying this book; well, that was the English language. When he was on the street, well, that was another language.

FRANK GARIBOLDI

"The word was *nothing* not *nothin'*. Ya gotta pronounce the *g*'s delicately, and the *t*'s had to be pronounced either softly or specifically, no harsh *s*'s. Hell, that could ruin the whole mood. All the words have a meaning, or they connect one word to another and each word stands by itself, yet each word blends with the next and the next, and together, they convey a message, one of love or sadness or desire. The words convey all kinds of messages, all short ones. In 2 to 3 minutes ya' have to say it all and ya' have to leave those people out there hangin' on to your every word. Man, don't let 'em go. Swing with the word or glide with it, look at them, look in their eyes, don't be afraid. They need you and you need them."

Chapter Three

Dolly

He paused to go forward, but his mind went into reverse and went all the way back.

Now he was in his bedroom as a teenager, alone, very much alone. "Being an only child is not the greatest thing in the world. It is rather lonely. You don't have anybody to bounce things off. An older brother would have been good, even a sister or even somebody younger. The guys outside, shit, they have their own problems and yours are different. What a blast to be able to talk with a brother or sister about Mom or Dad. Man, they were a pair. She controlled everything, and he didn't say a word, not even a peep out of him.

"Who do you talk to? Yeh, I got a lot of stuff. I always had money and clothes. Shit, clothes, pants, shirts, all I wanted and I must'a had 20 pair of pants. I was a clotheshorse. I guess I still am.

"I couldn't talk to the ol' man and tryin' to talk to her was like tryin' to talk to a wall. She always had the first word and the last one and the one in between. And this was not only with me but also with everybody else. She was a real politician. She was never at a loss for words. She shudda' been the mayor of Hoboken. She had the moxie. She had the balls."

He picked up a piece of gum, unwrapped it, and began to chew, slowly savoring that first bite, then he turned around from this wall of fame and books, still holding on to the *Elements of Style,* and began to walk across the room over to the large window that overlooked the back lawn where the in ground pool was and all the chairs and tables surrounding the water.

As he raised his right arm placing his elbow on the wall above his head, he began to think about the old neighborhood.

"Hoboken, what a dinky town! But back then that was all I had and that was my world. I had my own bike, and I was the first guy to have a car. Shit, and I always had money. You could buy a lot of stuff if you have money, and I was always buyin' stuff for the guys. And that's how you got the girlz."

Frank had always been a ladies' man. The ladies began way back then when he was a teenager. Since he had money, he was always dressed to the "nines." The smile, the blue eyes, and a few bucks in his pocket, and that's all he needed with the girls. There was always a lot of flirting going on, and then there were times when some of that flirting became more serious and he would wind up in bed with one or two of them. He never did stop doing that, getting into bed with one or two of them. The ladies became part of his life.

Frank had been up several hours now, and the feeling that had been with him since he was a teenager began to come over him. He was not sure what was happening, but he always followed his instincts. He had been feeling this for so many years that now this became second nature to him. Soon, he walked across the room and walked into a small room. This room was in the corner of His Room, but large enough to contain a wardrobe of clothes and an area to change into those clothes. There was also a small bathroom at one end. This was his changing room.

There he slowly began to take off the clothes he was

wearing and put on a new set of underwear, slacks, and shirt.

This need for change had been with him since he was a teenager, and he remembered doing his "changing" even then.

He never thought much about the changing. It was simply a part of him. He remembered that even on stage when he had a break, before the next song was to start, he had to quickly remove his clothes and put on all fresh clothing. They probably thought he was nuts, but he could care less. He remembered the guys in Tommy's band calling him Lady Macbeth.

He *had* to change.

The clothes were almost ripped off his body and thrown in a pile or just thrown anywhere for his manager to pick up.

And washing his hands? He always seemed to be near running water to keep his hands clean. *Did I get that from my mother?* he thought. *I don't know why the hell I change, but I can't stand dirt on me. The dirt feels creepy. There's nothin' like a clean set of duds on ya to make ya feel good all over. So screw them all!* he thought with emphasis.

Changing clothes had become second nature to him. Without haste, he changed into a new set of clothes. He was almost tempted to begin dressing for the show, but he knew that was too early.

Frank was an impeccable dresser. His clothing was the finest that money could buy. All his clothing, slacks, shirts, jackets, and tuxedos, were made especially for him, and they had to fit just so. He knew that clothing made the man, and as far as he was concerned, his clothing meant a lot to him.

He also did a lot of standing, to not wrinkle his clothes. He always wanted to give the correct image.

As he stood there looking in the full-wall mirror for any

imperfections, he thought about Dolly, his mother. She was just as clean as he was. Her house was impeccable. Everything was shiny and clean. Everything was in place, and if you moved something there was always hell to pay. Even when they sat down to dinner, only the three of them or with company, she always kept after the table—no crumbs, no spots. Perfect! She was obsessed with cleanliness.

He must have gotten that from her. "What the hell!" he exclaimed. "I feel better clean than lookin' like a slob."

He did not know how many articles of clothing he had, but he knew he had closets of them in New York, London, and here at home. He never was concerned about clothing. That was taken care of by the valet who went everywhere he went.

Albert was good, but as he reminisced, he thought George was the best. *George Jacobs,* he thought. *I wonder whatever happened to him.*

He dressed first with clean underwear, then found the right shirt to go with the slacks that had a crease you could cut bread with.

Frank was a natural with clothes; he had that certain instinct that he knew what color matched and what shirt to wear with what pair of slacks. He wasn't sure where that instinct came from, but being a clotheshorse certainly helped in the dressing room and in the world that he existed in.

As he sat in the chair to put on new clean socks and a new pair of matching alligator shoes that perfectly complemented the slacks and shirt, he stretched back and thought about George Jacobs who had been his valet, chef, cook, and bottle washer. You name it, and George was always there for him.

Frank had stolen George from Swifty Lazar. Just like that.

One minute George was working for Swifty, and the next minute he was working for Frank. *Man, that was a real deal,* thought Frank. "I just doubled his salary, and George was workin' for me. He could do everything, and every time I needed him he was there. Why did he leave me? Oh yea! I caught him with the skinny one, Mia. Now, that was a disaster. All she ever wanted was my bones. It shoulda' neva' happened. Shit, I was old enough to be her father. She was a good kid! Where the hell is she now?"

Frank was sitting up in the chair, looking around his dressing room and yet, his mind was traveling back to the beginning and over and through and then back again over this life of his.

Last night had put him out of sorts. Frank was a perfectionist following in his mother's path. He needed things done just so and no one could tell him what to do. The song "My Way" was perfectly written for him.

His perfectionism came about from being alone, from being abandoned as a child. Now Frank was always with his parents, but primarily raised by his grandmother. His abandonment came from the fact that Mom and Dad were never around. They were always working, and he always had to look out for himself. He had to make his own decisions. He really had no one to talk with, to get advice from, so good or bad, he took his own way. He would make his own decision because as far as he was concerned nobody really cared for him.

Well, his mother gave him all kinds of gifts and money, but she never showed him any kind of love. She was always involved with somebody or something. She was always trying to "get ahead" or "showing those neighbors" that we were as good as them. The Irish did have the neighborhood sewed up, but she was going to show them a thing or two. She was never around for him. Like Frank said earlier, he never knew when she was going to hit him or kiss him. She did this until the day she died. Oh, she was proud of him, all right, but she was the boss, and she let everybody know that. When she came in, she took over the room. Her presence alone demanded that, and when she spoke she let everyone know who was in charge. Frank was second; everybody was second. She became number one, and she never let anyone forget, not even her Frankie.

As Frank remembered her, he slowly folded his arms across his chest as if trying to keep her away from him and yet wanting her love so badly that his mouth became dry and his breathing came in short gulps.

He shook himself, let his arms down, and continued his reverie.

He could never trust her. She only bought him things to buy his love. And the old man! Shit! Well, he just followed Dolly and did whatever she told him to do. She was the one who finally, through her connections, got the old man a job in the fire department. His father was always either looking for work or working a job here or there until Mom finally was able to pull enough strings to get him a job in the fire department. He tried to be a father; damn, he tried, but with a wife like that, I don't know how he even stayed with her.

She was the king of the hill, the top rooster. Nobody, but nobody, told her what to do. She was mixed up with a lot of politicians, and I don't think they ever were able to control her. But she was smart, quite a bright lady. She was able to speak all the Italian dialects, and she was always there for all Italians in the neighborhood. She was able to swing votes any way the politicians wanted her to. She worked for the political machine, and she was good at what she did, and best of all, she did like to help people.

That combination of politics and love of people carried over into Frank's career and lifestyle.

Frank was the one who got the short end of the stick. She was never around for him. Grandma took care of him. His father, well, he had his problems, and Mom, well, she was queen of the political hill, and she never let anyone forget that. She was only around to administer punishment, and then, in order to make up for all the parental deficiencies, she always gave him money—money for clothes or money to treat his friends. Frank always became the center of attraction. His closet was always filled with the best slacks, shirts, and sports coats. He was the first in the neighborhood to have a car.

He had all these things, and yet he had nothing. All he really wanted was a mother and father that he could talk to and count on. They were never there for him.

His mother also dabbled as a midwife, and the abortion stories about her haunted him growing up. The kids were always throwing those stories in his face. He would have to fight or run. He became a loner.

Frank remembered that one night he and his mother became a little closer. The night she finally conceded to him his right to sing.

Frank had come home around two o'clock in the morning, 13 days before Christmas, December 12, 1933. He had just celebrated his 18th birthday. Frank would never forget that night.

He slowly closed the door and silently crossed over into

the kitchen to get a glass of milk and a piece of leftover birthday cake that was under cover on the lower kitchen cabinets.

As he flipped on the switch, there she was. Mom. Just sitting there, waiting in her nightgown and robe and with a yardstick in her hand.

Grandma was always using that yardstick on some neighbor's dress or pants. She either raised them or lowered them; the yardstick became part of Grandma's hand.

His mother got up and began to scream and holler as soon as she saw him, using the choicest words of the gutter. She knew them all. As she yelled and screamed at him, the yardstick became like a baton, and she, the orchestra leader.

Frank was stunned at the whole scene.

As she screamed at him the yardstick was being used for emphasis, being waved and sometimes slammed on the kitchen table. She also began to tap the floor with the stick, and for emphasis, bringing it down sharply to the floor when she wanted to make a specific point.

Frank could not get over this. He silently looked at her and kept glancing at the yardstick as she waved it all over, not wanting to be the object of this wrath or the object of the stick.

She had always thrown tantrums, but this one was a beauty. She was trying to make him see the error of his ways. Singing was no good. He was going to turn out to be a bum, and she emphasized this by calling him a "fuckin' bum."

"Look at you," she screamed. "You're gonna turn out to be a fuckin' bum. You quit school! No job! All ya wanna do is sing. Dat's no good! No son of mine is gonna do dat." As she screamed the words at him the yardstick whirled in her hand and kept getting closer and closer to his head.

She continued to bring up his friends and the nice jobs they had as bricklayers, carpenters, cooks, waiters. She even mentioned Al who had become a fireman.

"Why can't you be like dem?" she screamed, and for emphasis she swung the yardstick over her head and sent "her baton" crashing down on Frank's shoulder. The yardstick split in two.

They looked at each other astounded at this occurrence. Frank cracked a little smile while his mother in shock, began to cry. They reached out to each other, embraced, and as they held on to each other, they were both sobbing as she let go of the split yardstick.

As the broken yardstick clattered to the floor they both pushed out their arms from that warm embrace and smiled at each other. She slowly raised her right arm and began to caress the right side of Frank's face with her right hand and softly said, "*Ti amo* - I love you!" to her only child.

They remained this way for a few moments, both looking at each other with tears streaming down their faces. Frank slowly placed his head on her shoulder, and Dolly embraced him again.

They remained that way for a few moments longer, mother and son, seeking love from each other.

When they released each other, she went over to the cake, cut him a big piece, placed that big slice on a plate, and waved him over to the kitchen table. She walked over to the silverware drawer, pulled out a fork, and reached up to the cabinet for a glass. She then walked over to the refrigerator, pulled out the milk, and poured him a glassful. She then walked over to the table, arranged all these items in front of Frank, and sat down across from him. She then waited for him to speak.

Frank could not remember the last time his mother had given him this much attention. Grandma was always taking care of him.

As he sat there with his coat still on, he began to pour his heart out. Singing was all that he ever wanted to do. He was going to be the next Bing Crosby, he needed to practice, he needed a few breaks. Frank explained that he was now singing in some saloons in town, and some of his friends were getting together to try out for the Major Bowes Amateur Radio Program. They had a good chance of winning.

He pleaded his case while wolfing down the cake and gulping the milk. He almost came to tears trying to make her understand that this was his deep down desire. He had to become the premier singer of his day. He had to make his dream happen. He explained he was taking voice lessons from an ex-opera singer who told him that he should use a microphone so he could practice and learn how to use his voice in the best way possible.

He explained how Quinlan, his voice teacher, thought that Frank had a chance because of his passion for music. Quinlan said Frank needed a microphone because his voice was a little soft.

When he stopped talking, Dolly only looked at him rather vaguely. She then rose from her chair, went over to him, reached out, and pulled his head onto her chest and softly and tenderly she said in Italian, "*Figlio mio*—my son." And gently kissed the top of his head.

She then released him and walked out of the kitchen, went up the stairs and into her bedroom.

The next day when Frank came home, on his bed he found a complete and expensive handheld microphone set with amplifier sitting on his bed.

As the scene came back to him, he began to cry softly. Sobbing gently, he remembered this one event that, whether she liked the singing idea or not, she tried to give him a "push" in his direction. That gesture was the first time she gave in to his dream, and that could have been the last.

Dolly never gave into his becoming a singer and was always expecting the "shoe to drop." Yet, she gave him the chance. She gave him her okay to "make it or break it."

He remembered being raised by his grandmother, Dolly's mother. Now there was a good lady. As Frank remembered her she was always old, the white hair, the wrinkled face, but straight as a pin and full of energy. Man, she had enough energy for the whole family put together. She was always on the move. Just like her daughter, and he had that same energy.

Grandma "Nona" was the one who made him breakfast and fixed his lunch. She was always there when he came home from school and most nights made supper for the two of them, Frankie and her.

They did not talk too much to each other. She only spoke her Italian dialect and Frank never spoke the language. He only understood the words, and basically only understood her. His parents had come here as kids, and they could speak the dialect of their parents, Dolly from northern Italy, and his father from southern Italy. Dolly was able to master all the Italian dialects and that was what made her so good in the job she performed for the political party in the Hoboken area.

Dolly could speak all the dialects; help all the neighbors;

therefore, bring in all the votes. Dolly had the personality for politics, and Frank followed in her footsteps.

As far as Frank was concerned, he wanted his mother home, just like some of the other moms in the neighborhood, but his father never could hold down a job and the economic depression was even worse for the old man. Dolly went political, and she was the number-one breadwinner in the family. And when you came into her house you always knew that this was *her* house, no ifs, ands, or buts.

Frank became a lot like Mom. The room he walked in was always his room, and you knew that, no ifs, ands, or buts.

Frank wanted the same adulation as his mother received from the neighbors, and although he rebelled against her he was really a lot like her. Her personality, her temper, the desire to be somebody, her aloofness, her aggressiveness, these were all her traits.

Well, all of these traits, plus a few more that he picked up along the way became the man Sinatra. This is what formed him. The world stage became his playground while she remained in the political area of Hoboken.

In those days women were just beginning to take part in politics, and Dolly was right in the middle of that beginning. Her gift was feeling the pain of her neighbors, reaching out to them through politics, and then getting them to vote for her party, therefore, keeping her party in office. She would do anything to keep "the stinkin' Irish" out of office.

Dolly was consumed with herself.

When you're alone most of the time, the only one that you can count on is you. You have to make all the decisions, good or bad. And you have to live with them. You cannot go crying to someone else about those decisions because no one else really cares. You are always on your own. You learn to trust no one, only your own instincts.

Frank learned to live by his instincts, and for most of his life they were good and he did very well for himself.

Frank had been making those decisions, since he was a teenager, and he had a strong will, an inheritance from his mother. He was always determined to become a big star, to be the next Crosby. His dream was always to be the personality as he was now, known the world over. And he had always done everything his way. The only time he may have begged a little, actually, he begged a lot, was in getting the Maggio role. He even asked for, and received, the lowest salary that the union allowed for that role, but he was still fighting for what he thought was the right thing for him.

Being alone taught him all of that. He had hardened himself against the world. He was truly a loner. Sometimes even in a crowded room he could go off by himself and be alone. He needed all the adulation that he received from his audience. That is what nourished him, that is, what kept him alive; that is what kept him going. No one or no thing was as good as that audience to sustain him to keep the juices flowing. He owed a lot to that audience, and last night he had let them down.

"I was a jerk, a shit head last night," he shouted out to the mirror in front of him. "I owe those people. Without dem I'm nothin'. How da hell did I let that happin'? Well, I'm throwin' out those fuckin' pills!!" he exclaimed as he rose from the chair and went out into his room again.

He felt a little better now that he had put on a new set of

clothes and washed his hands. He had put all the blame on the pills and had decided to be rid of them as soon as he could get his hands on them.

As he strode back into the room he looked around. The Oscar was the central attraction in this room, yet the room contained many other awards and citations. Frank had been honored by so many people and countries that he needed a room this size to keep all the trophies, plaques, scrolls, and the memorabilia that he had acquired over the last 50 years of entertaining the world. He needed all this memorabilia; his ego demanded it.

He was especially proud of all the charitable benefits that he had performed in over those years. The donations from those benefits reached into the millions.

But for Frank the money was not the object; the charity itself made him do all those events. Frank never kept anything for himself when he worked on these events.

He always showered his friends and children with gifts, many of them unexpected.

The gifts from the heart made him special. When Sammy was in the accident that took his eye and almost wiped out a marvelous career from a very talented man, Frank was the one who not only paid for the doctor bills but the talks that he had with Sam were the principal reason that Sammy came back, or the time that Buddy Rich, his enemy from the beginning of his career, wanted to start a band. The only person who would loan him money was Frank. Or when Louie Prima was in the hospital in a coma and had no money because he always gambled his money away, the only one around to pay all his hospital bills was Frank.

There were other acts of charity that sometimes you never heard about, the ones in the newspaper or on the radio or TV. The person who was hurt on the job or had a terrible accident or had some other terrible illness, that was the person who would be the recipient of Frank's generosity.

Those kinds of trophies were not on the wall, but they were all part of this man called Frank Sinatra.

And yet, there were times that you would not have wanted to be called his friend for the stupid and ugly things that he did. He reacted just like his mother. She would hit him, then wrap her arms around him and love him to death. That's what Frank would do; react in a rush, and then buy gifts to apologize, never using words.

Journalists were and still are his number-one nemesis, and yet, there were some that he treated with much love and consideration like Walter Winchell and Pete Hamill.

Chapter Four
Work Sheets

His rage against journalists was well known and well documented. Dorothy Kilgallen and Lee Mortimer always caused Frank "accida," as he would express that feeling. He may have expressed his journalistic feeling more violently and did so one night with Mortimer. That altercation cost Frank quite a few bucks and almost landed him in jail. Fortunately, he listened to Louis B. Mayer and settled out of court.

He had mellowed over the years and did pick some form of media to showcase his life and views. He had done a good interview with Walter Cronkite expressing himself and his lifestyle. The interview was like a sparring match. Walter throwing some punches, and Frank blocking and backpedaling. All in all, the interview was a good one, each holding his own and Frank coming away from the interview without too many scratches.

But Walter Winchell and Pete Hamill, they were different. When Walter Winchell was the talk of the town in New York City, they would find a "water hole" where they could loosen up and talk about anything and everything. Of course, Walter was true to his trade, and if something came up that needed to be printed he did so, but in most cases, they were skewed toward Frank's side.

Pete was another journalist that Frank trusted. They also spent many nights together in various drinking holes, Jilly's or

Toot Shors' being some of the favorite watering holes. While the latter was too wide open, Jilly's did have a back room for more privacy. They also spent many nights driving through the "caverns" of New York City just being friends, talking about nothing in particular or politics, a favorite subject, or lost loves or people, those people that paid to get into the shows that Frank performed in and that Pete wrote for. They both had a feeling for those people. The "little" guy. As Frank called him, "The poor slob that really worked for his money, and then puts it up to see me in a show."

While driving back from one of those shows one night, Frank had expressed why he had no racial issues with the black man. He had grown up in Hoboken where he had experienced ethnic slurs against the Italians in the neighborhood. He had run from the Irish guys in the neighborhood when they promised him a "fuckin' beatin'" if he ever showed up in their part of town again. He had been in the brawls and seen the blood of his friends, and some of his own, all over the street.

He had read about the hangings of all those Italians in New Orleans in 1891. Eleven were tried for murder, and the jury had acquitted eight and no verdict on the other three. There was simply no evidence. Yet, the people of New Orleans stormed the jail, pulled out the eleven men, and hung them from lampposts, only because they were Italian and the people had connected them to the Mafia.

He knew the feeling of being racially profiled because of his Italian heritage. He had seen this kind of profiling face-to-face in the clubs he worked concerning the blacks, the Jews, the Italians. Color or race did not make a difference. If they wanted you out you were out. Whenever he could, he would stand up for the black man. Once or twice they came close to closing the show. He would not bend in any way on that position. And he did this in the early forties when he was just beginning his career. This stand for blacks could have been the end of his career. And even though he was begged, "to give up this stand on blacks and let somebody else be the hero," he never once bent on this idea of freedom for all.

Back in the forties he was presented with an award for the short film *The House I Live In*. This was something he was really proud of. The Oscar was his showpiece, his comeback. The Oscar told the world, "I'm back; I can still do it."

The House I Live In award, well, that really defined him as a human being. That said, "I belong to this world." There was never much talk about God in his life, but this award squared him away with his fellow man.

Yet, *The House I Live In* award was not in the place of honor like the Oscar. It was something he cherished more than anything else that he had been given during his lifetime in show business. That "House" award made him a humanitarian. It exemplified who Frank was, someone who loved people and who would give his life for those people.

With all his bravado, *The House I Live In* award was off to the side in this special room of his. Only he knew that he would give his life and career to stand up for all that the award stood for. He was of Italian descent, yet he was American first, and prejudice, as far as he was concerned, was worth fighting, and even dying, for.

"Damn last night," he said out loud, as his voice vibrated around the room. This was really turning his insides out. As he slowly made his way to the large Steinway piano that was placed in a corner, yet drew as much attention as did his Oscar, he said again, "Damn last night."

"Where the fuck is last night's program?" Frank was very meticulous about all the songs he sang. He did not rehearse. Most of the songs he was singing had been with him for 30, 40 years, some songs, since the beginning of his career. Some of these songs made him who he was, the ballad singer, the singer that all those others tried to emulate but never could. Oh, yes, some of them sold more albums, records, or CDs than he did, but none of them could give the same feeling, the same warmth, the same nuance to words and music that Frank could do. Frank had followed Quinlan's advice. These songs became his. They belonged to Frank Sinatra.

He was the man to copy and emulate, and no one had even come close.

Before any appearance, Frank would pick out the songs. He would review some 40 or 50 songs, then pick out the 10 or 11 that were going to be used for the show or a new CD. Many times an arranger had an idea for the show or CD and would suggest songs for him to sing. No one dared tell him to sing this song or that one. One could only "suggest," and Frank would consider and agree or disagree and that was that.

He was very attentive to some arrangers more that others. Nelson Riddle was probably his favorite. Nelson had been the arranger when he changed record companies from Columbia to Capital. Nelson had suggested some songs that were perfect for Frank's voice. He had met Frank after *From Here to Eternity*, after Frank had hemorrhaged his vocal chords, and after Frank's romance with Ava.

FRANK GARIBOLDI

Nelson had known about Frank's temperament and nothing had changed when they met and for all the years they were to work together. Frank was always in charge, and you never knew how the music session was going to work out, but they respected each other and Nelson could only suggest songs or ideas for an album. Frank knew what he wanted, and Nelson, in his arranging, always got the best from him. Nelson always said, "Frank can't read music, but he has a golden ear."

The vocal chords fiasco which almost closed down Frank's career also strengthened them, gave them a special timbre, that special resonance and quality that he never had as a young singer. Oh, he was good, but the vocal chord fiasco was a blessing in disguise. Someone was certainly looking after Frank.

His romance with Ava gave him the reason to sing that way—to brood, to feel the pain, to cry with no tears, to bare his soul to the world so the world could walk in his shoes and feel all the pain themselves.

Gordon Jenkins, Don Costa, Quincy Jones, and other arrangers used their talent and suggestions to enhance Frank's career. But his voice, a voice that had stood the test of time, was a pure gift and Frank knew. He nurtured the voice and was very mindful of his voice at all times. Smoking, drinking, and late hours did not help, yet he did all he could to look after the voice.

"Where the hell is that program?" he shouted again making his voice vibrate and echo throughout the room. As he sat on the piano stool, he moved some papers and some song sheets and found his work sheets for last night's performance.

Now Frank had never learned to play the piano, but through all the years with his favorite music, he could play a few chords and finger a tune, but most of all, he was best at the lyrics. This is what he excelled at, the lyrics. He had learned from John Quinlan that the lyrics were the soul of the song and the interpreter of those lyrics gave the song life and brought happiness and joy or sadness to the listener. The singer of this music's lyrics held the listener in the palm of his hand. The singer connected music of the composer, words of the lyricist, and the balance of the arranger into a masterpiece . . . or a catastrophe. They did become his songs—Frank Sinatra. No one cared about the writer or the lyricist. Only Frank singing the songs mattered. John was right.

Frank always looked to make a masterpiece. He had learned well, not only from the teacher but also from listening to singers whom he thought were the best, Bing Crosby, Ella Fitzgerald, and Billie Holliday. His heart had been broken many times in his lifetime, especially by women—his mother, Ava.

All this and more made Frank Sinatra the balladeer, the crooner, the saloon singer. His dedication to the songs he picked, the time spent reviewing the lyrics were all that make up Frank Sinatra, the singer. The time spent living the lyrics added to the mystique.

All you have to do is listen to a Sinatra ballad and you know and feel the pain and anguish of a man who has suffered, a man who can feel the pain and express that pain in his music. And then conversely, he can fill the room with joy and happiness with a song of cheer, a song of goodwill.

In other words, there is only one interpreter of this music, "his music" as they have come to call the songs he sings—Frank Sinatra.

"Now I got the work sheets," he said in an exasperated tone as he picked up a bundle of papers. "Where the hell are the final cuts? Where the hell is last night's show?"

"Ahh," he sighed, "there they are."

The work sheets were right on top of all the song sheets for the show at the Universal Amphitheatre.

They were not in the order of the show, just randomly picked as the tunes that he would perform during his stay at Universal. The conductor or Bill Miller, his pianist for over 30 years, would then place them in order, and Frank would have the final say before the first show began. Years ago he would rehearse with the band, only once, but recently he had stopped doing that. The songs were embedded in his body; they were part of his soul.

Only last night, he thought, *what happened last night?*

He thought about last night. He had come to the theatre alone about 1 hour before the show was to begin. He immediately went on to the stage just to get a feel, just to know the stage. As many times as he had been on stage, especially on this one, the first night of the first show was always important to him. He had to get there a little early just to walk around to kind of get his bearings. He enjoyed walking up and down the stage reviewing some of the things he was going to say, but most of the time these words would come out spontaneously. He had been here before; he had been doing this for over 50 years.

The stage was just as he remembered. Smooth, clean, and not waxy, no slipping or tripping here. In fact, the floor seemed perfect to him.

The band was already there, each musician in his place, and the conductor for this whole run was to be his son, Frank Jr.

He thought about his son and their relationship, which was better than the one he had with his dad, but was not as good as he had with his daughters. Was the reason because they were women and understood him better or that the words came easier with his daughters? Over the last 10–15 years, he had tried to get closer to Frank Jr., but Frank never felt right. Frank always thought he was pressing the issue.

Frank loved his son very much, but had a difficult time expressing himself. Frank would rave about how good a conductor his son was, which was the truth. Frank Jr. had learned well. Frank Jr. had tried singing years ago, but that proved very difficult following in this icon's shoes. Frank Jr. loved music, so he did the next best thing, went to school for arranging and conducting, and that proved to be the best part of his musical talents.

Frank Jr. knew his dad's music inside and out, and even his moods. That was important to help interpret the music for a night's performance. Frank Jr. was good at what he did.

Frank did not want to have the same relationship with his son that he had with his dad, which was practically nothing!

Frank had to work at this relationship with his son, and he was never comfortable with the situation, at least until many years later. Even Nancy, who knew Frank better than anyone else, had begged him not to do the same thing that his parents had done to him. Nancy was always after him to reach out to Frankie Jr. "Don't let this issue become the same way as you and Dolly. Don't lose him," Nancy would beg.

His being on the road most of the time, his massive commitments, his work and social habits, all of these, and some that he made up in his own head, kept him from really getting to know his son and his daughters, for that matter.

But Frank had tried to have a better relationship with his son than the one he had with his father. He remembered that one night he waited for Frank Jr. to arrive home from a singing engagement. They had talked for a few hours with Frank doing most of the talking. The night became surreal because he remembered the night that Dolly waited for him, only this time Frank did not bring a yardstick.

Frank explained the relationship he had with his father and did not want to have the same one with his son. Frank told Frank Jr. that he had no relationship with his father. Frank's father was a good man and worked very hard when he was given a job to do. Frank's mom was always giving his dad a job to do. She is the one who kept him at work. Frank's father was not a shirker, but he never had the drive or ambition that Frank's mother had. And his father and Frank never spoke to each other about anything that mattered. Frank also knew that his father always thought that show business was the pits and that Frank would some day fail and then he would have to get a real job. Frank wanted to have this talk with his son so that Frank Jr. and he could have a better relationship. Frank also went on to explain and apologize for some of his actions toward Frank Jr.

The evening became a father/son pact. With women this is almost automatic, but men have to shake hands, embrace, and almost write it in blood. "Let's not stop talking to each other. If we have a problem, let's get it out, put everything on the table." They promised love to each other, and Frank promised his son that nothing that Frank Jr. could do or say would ever break that resolve of their father/son relationship. They loved each other.

At the end of that long conversation, with Frank doing most of the talking, they both agreed to never let anything get in the way of their relationship. They agreed to put everything on the table if one or the other had something to say to the other.

After the "talk," things seemed to improve a bit and they did put everything on the table once in a while. Frank's relationship with his son improved, but their schedules and Frank's divorce from Nancy kept him away from the family. Being divorced was not a great way to build a relationship. Both men needed each other, but they never could find a way to come closer. Only in their work together could you see the love they had for each other.

Frank knew what he had with his son was better than the relationship he had with his father, and many times he silently thanked Nancy for that conversation she had with him. Yet, Frank thought at times that he could have done more. Could this have been the guilt of not being there for some of the small things in Frank Jr.'s life, the games and the concerts? He could have done more he thought regretfully, but you cannot change the past.

Frank's daughters, as he surmised, were easier to love, perhaps because they were girls and thought and acted differently. They were able to express themselves more. Even though Frank was a man's man, he always had a way with women, and his daughters were no exception. He could talk to them for hours about one thing or another. He also seemed to be able to please them more with his gifts. He was never buying their love. He just always wanted to shower his children with gifts and did that as often as possible.

Frank thought about this a little longer, and then put Frank Jr. and the girls aside. He picked up a mint and the show papers and the music and lyrics to the show that he had screwed up on last night.

"Now, let's do a little rehearsal!" he exclaimed to no one in particular. The house was silent. Everyone was out, and he was alone in his room. He sat down on the piano bench and began to review the show's music and lyrics.

Frank always tried to make his shows something special. He loved his audience, and he wanted nothing more than to please them. He wanted "to get under their skin," so to speak. He wanted them to feel the music in the same way that he did, to feel good, to feel happy, to feel sad. He wanted his music and his voice to be remembered by them forever.

Frank did not have to think these thoughts. They were just there. He knew he was given a gift to please his audience, to please that one person out there who needed to listen to his songs and feel the mood of the music.

That one person to make the words part of his being.

That one person out there who only wanted to be entertained.

That one person out there who had just fallen in love and wanted to be lifted up to the heights of that love and needed Frank's music to be able to express to himself and to that girl who had just said yes to his request for marriage.

That one person who had just been turned down and needed Frank's voice to soothe the pain.

He knew the effect that he had on his audience because he could feel "it" in his inner being. He could not explain why, but he knew that "it" was there, some special gift given to him, and at times like these, he thought about God and thanked him for the gift.

Frank and God had not been too close. His parents had brought him to the usual Catholic things, Holy Communion and Confirmation. He had married Nancy in a Catholic Church, Our Lady of Sorrows in Jersey City.

But for all intents and purposes, God and church were not part of his life. He had done a lot of praying to get the Maggio part, and then later, just before he had been nominated for the Oscar, there were some more prayers. He prayed the time he lost his voice and thought his career was over. He also had done a lot of praying when his son had been kidnapped.

And since Mom was killed in that plane accident he had come back to his roots as a Catholic and gone to church a little more frequently.

Yet, Frank knew that the gift of his voice came from God.

Frank shook these thoughts out of his head and came back to the reality of last night's fiasco.

"What a dumb shit I was last night. Trippin', not hittin' the high ones, and forgettin' words. This has got to stop! It's got to stop!" he shouted out into his room and the echo vibrated, came back to him, and gave him a chill that made him sit up straight and look around as if someone were there watching and observing his every move.

"Let's do it," he spoke to the piano as he began to finger the piano and slowly arrange the papers to review last night's show.

As he began to review the first number "You are the Sunshine of My Life," he thought about the band and the stage crew. They were all good musicians. Some of them he had known for years. There was no doubt about his son. As conductor, Frank Jr. was one of the best, and he knew Frank's musical moods inside and out. The stage crew had done their jobs to perfection. Lights, special effects, all went well.

He had goofed. He had messed this up himself, and when this had to do with his music and his performance on stage, Frank was perfection personified. "I really fucked it up last night; now let's go over this from top to bottom."

1) "You Are the Sunshine of My Life"—Music and lyrics by Stevie Wonder
2) "You Go to My Head"—Music, J. Coots; lyric, H. Gillespie
3) "You Make Me Feel so Young"—Music, Josef Myrow; lyrics, Mack Gordon
4) "Night and Day"—Music and lyrics by Cole Porter
5) "Soliloquy"—Music, R. Rodgers; lyrics, O. Hammerstein
6) "You Will Be My Music"—Music and lyrics by Joseph Raposo
7) "They Can't Take That Away from Me"—Music and lyrics, George and Ira Gershwin
8) "New York! New York!"—Music, John Kander; lyrics, Fred Ebb
9) "Embraceable You"—Music and lyrics by George and Ira Gershwin
10) "I've Got you Under My Skin"—Music and lyrics by Cole Porter
11) "One for My Baby"—Music, Harold Arlen; lyrics, Johnny Mercer

That was the show.

Some arrangements were kept the same. Nelson Riddle's were always kept. Frank liked that style. Nelson knew him inside and out.

He used Don Costa whenever he could. But the other songs he left up to Frank Jr., who knew his dad as well as anyone else and could arrange the music to Frank's inner moods. Bill Miller, his pianist from forever, was always there, leading, coaxing, never out of step; just being there at Frank's side was enough.

Chapter Five

Retirement

As Frank reviewed the show, he saw that everything was put together well, almost as he would have wanted. He, however, did not have enough time to put this particular show together because of commitments he had on the East Coast. The fact was that he had arrived only about 3 hours before this show opened. He barely had enough time to shower, shave, and get dressed for this one. He had left immediately for the theatre to relax a little and get acquainted with the stage. Still, that was not what would have caused the terrible things he had done last night. He was about to correct that situation right now.

He knew that Barbara and his daughters, Nancy and Tina, had proposed retirement, but that was out of the question. He loved the stage too much. He loved those people too much. He could never retire. Sometimes he could see himself doing the big number and dropping dead right on the stage. Just like Crosby who died on the golf course.

What a way to end a career, he thought silently. *The grand exit.*

As the thought of "is it all over," popped into his head, a kind of uneasiness straightened him right up. "This can't be the time for me to call it quits," he ruminated.

He slowly began to rise from the piano stool. And then abruptly sat down again. He could feel his face become flush as the thought of his career being over raced through his mind.

"Over! Over! It can't be!" he shouted. "I just came back from Washington singin' for the president. No screwups dere."

Now he was really getting warm. He could feel the heat all over his body as this thought of retirement soared through his whole body making him very uneasy. His mind flashed *heart attack,* but he quickly dismissed that thought.

"You know I've been doin' this over 50 years. Maybe now, maybe now is the time to let go," he whispered. "I remember doing it once, but dat was hell. I was drivin' everybody nuts. What a fiasco! Sittin' around, paintin', goin' to nightclubs, grand openings, travelin'. Shit, dat was fuckin' for da birds," he screamed as his voice reverberated around the room.

But that was 20 years ago, and I was too fuckin' young to retire.

As the voice in his head subsided, the clamminess left him and his body began to cool down. The thought of changing again entered his mind, but he thought no, too close to showtime. The pressure gauge in his body was beginning to release him.

As he calmly surveyed his room from the vantage point of the piano stool, he began to relax, and then that smile crossed his face, and as he nodded negatively, he emphatically and calmly spoke these words, "No, it's not over yet!"

This was something that he had screwed up. He was not paying attention to business. He had to take more time to review. Still, he could not figure why this was happening to him. As he looked over the show tunes, he realized that these tunes had been sung by him many, many times over. There was no reason for screwing up the words. And stumbling over nothing, what the hell was *that* all about, he wondered.

"It's the damn pills," he shouted as he slammed his hand on

the piano. "The pills! I've got to get rid of them or cut back on them. What the hell am I taking them for?

"I'm still in pretty good shape for 75. I could cut back on smokin'. Maybe less drinkin'. Aw, shit! What the hell would that do? What good is life if you can't have some fun goin' through? It's the damn pills. And not enough reviewin'. Let's look at this thing!"

As Frank sat down and looked over the whole show, he realized again that the show had been put together rather well. Some rhythm ballads, the big number could have been put down a notch or two, the ballads were dispersed in good places, and the saloon song at the end was right there where "It's Quarter To Three" was supposed to be.

This was a good show!

Frank always did his shows as an actor, doing a one-man show. There had to be a beginning, a middle, and an end. Frank Jr. and Bill Miller were aware of this. I'm sure many of the musicians who had played with him before knew the same thing. This was not rocket scientist stuff; this was Frank Sinatra doing the thing he loved the most, singing in front of an audience and giving everything, his body and soul.

The rhythm ballads were for the whole audience as was the big number, but the love ballads and the saloon song were for each individual person in the theatre. He brought the audience into his space one song at a time and one person at a time. The bouncy tunes, the love ballads, the big show number, then back to some ballads and a swing number or two; the music was all prepared to bring the audience into his space. This was the only time he did this; on the stage he opened himself up and bared his soul.

In all this he was the ultimate saloon singer, putting his heart on the line. He let the world know that he had been beat up and that he had been through some rough times emotionally. He shared his life with anyone who took the time to really listen. He became one of them.

Life was about the highs and lows and fighting your way through all the ugliness and all the joys. Frank had been through his own life, and he shared that life with everyone who wanted to hear and feel the pain or the joy.

He sang about everyone's dream.

Frank was able to showcase his life and right in front of an audience, his audience. They knew, and he knew. They wanted his music to wash over them and bring them to the reality of their lives.

They needed him as much as he needed them.

When the stage got dark, when the spotlight was only on him and the music softened, then he sang only for one person. Even though there were thousands of people there, only one person at a time heard him, felt the music and words go over and through him or her. Only one person at a time knew that he was singing only to him. Only one person at a time knew that those words were about all the stuff that she had been through, all that stuff that he had suffered through. This was magic! This was pure gift!

The best part was that Frank knew; he knew. This chemistry that Frank had been doing for over 50 years was not new to him. He knew what was in his soul and now, after 50 years, he knew he could never, never let go. He would rather be dead than give up on the audience. And the audience felt the same way. They both needed each other. They both wanted each other.

But one of them had screwed up last night. Frank!

"Retire! Who am I fuckin' kiddin'?" he blared and slapped his hand on the piano with such force that the piano trembled from the aftershock.

"Look at these songs," he spoke to no one in particular. "I've been singin' some of these forever. 'You Go to My Head,' 'Night and Day,' 'They Can't Take That Away from Me,' 'Embraceable You,' 'One for My Baby'—my God, I've been singin' dese forever," he said again as he slammed the "show" that he held in his hand on the piano keys, and they answered him back with a clank that echoed throughout the room.

"Why did I fuck up?" he lamented. "Now if I had done this on 'You Are the Sunshine of My Life,' or even 'New York, New York,' they are fairly new songs in my shows; maybe I could understand. But when I slip and trip and screw up on 'Night and Day,' 'Embraceable You,' and 'I've Got You under My Skin,' man, there's no excuse. None whatsoever." He continued to beat himself up with words.

He felt the pain of "screwing up." Making a mistake was not in his character. He had made some beauties in his lifetime but not on stage, not in front of these people he loved. This was uncalled for. This was outrageous. This was not Frank Sinatra! Frank was always at his best with a live audience. The stage is where he came alive, where the words, music, and everything in his being shouted out to the world—"It's me! It's me!" And Frank needed to be heard. He needed the world to listen to him. He needed the friendship and the love he received from that audience. He could not live without the love that the audience gave him.

This moment was like when you screw up in front of your

children for the first time. That is when they find out that you are mortal. That you can screw up just like them. Some of the shine comes off. That's what happened last night. He became mortal.

Then he stopped in the middle of his thoughts. His whole body shivered as the idea of retirement swept through him. "Da ya think it's time?" he whispered.

As this thought rolled roughly through his head, again a chill ran through his whole body causing him to come to a complete stop. The thought scared him. What would he do? His mind went back to the last time, and that was not a pleasant thing that had occurred. He had retired, and what a fiasco!

But he was now 75 years old. Life had taken a bite out of him. His body and voice were not as supple as they used to be. The aches and pains came more readily. He was drinking less, but now he was feeling the alcohol. Was this the time to let go? *Could* he let go?

He had always heard the expression, "When's the time to get married?" Was this the same thing? When's the time to retire?

"Hell, I've been doing this for over 50 years, bouncin' all over the place. One-night stands. Hell, it's been better lately; I get to pick and choose. That's a good thing. Could I stay home? What da hell would I do?"

"No! No! No!" he screamed while standing and waving his hands wildly over his head. "It's not time! It's not time!" he boomed out as the words reverberated around the room in a mad crescendo.

"It's not time!" he whispered softly as his body began to relax after this emotional outburst. The beating of his heart came back to normal. He bowed his head as his whole body began to relax, and he reached back to the piano and calmly sat down.

"It's not time," he whispered again, trying to put his mind to rest. But he had exerted himself, and his mind would not rest that quickly.

What *would* he do? Dean and Sammy were gone! Could he play golf every day like Dean loved to do? Shit! He never even liked the game that much; he only played for celebrity causes. Frank would say, "Thank God that's over" when he took off his golf shoes.

No! Golf was not for him.

Frank knew that the voice was not as good as 15 years ago, or even 5 years ago. Too much smoking and drinking. Too many late nights. What really was worrying him now was the memory loss. That was scary. Alzheimer's? Dementia?

As he continued to think about these things his whole body became warm, and then a chill shot right through him. He jumped up quickly and said in a hoarse whisper, "Could it be over? Is this it? I'm only 75. Shit, that's not old."

"What the hell am I gonna do?" He began to sit slowly on the stool, but then rose upright. His mind went blank for a few minutes as this awful situation of retiring and memory loss coursed through his mind and began to hurt his body. He could feel the pain right in his chest.

What *would* he do?

He could paint. Now that would be something. He had done that in his spare time and even tried painting the last time he "retired." In fact, some pictures came out fairly well. You know, flowers and stuff, some scenery. He was terrible with doing people, yet he had tried, and they did not come out too bad; not good either. Frank was always looking for perfection, always.

He could write the story of his life. He had been asked to do that many times, but he always resisted that idea. They could even make a movie. But who the hell would play him? He thought seriously about that one, and then as he shook his head emphatically no, his mind told him that there was no one out there who could do him justice.

What about taking on a cause? Do something like Jerry is doing with the kids or maybe traveling around and meeting new singers, entertainers. The ones that still hold on to the old songs, the old tunes. That really would be something to do, to find those people who would keep his music going.

Today's music is crap, he thought. *Maybe I could establish some kind of school to teach the "old music" and help bring together those singers and musicians who can still do and want to do the old ballads so that this music lives on forever.*

Now that was something that appealed to him.

Frank was now in a reverie as these thoughts of retiring with a cause circled his mind. He thought of people and places where he could start this school. Somewhere that could be a jump-off point to bring back the ballad and kill this rock 'n' roll crap.

Frank wanted to bring back the good music, the music that he loved.

As he continued to run with these thoughts, he suddenly stopped and realized deep down, this was not the time.

"I've got to go on," he whispered softly. "I've got to go on," he gently uttered. "It's not time," he said, putting that thought to rest.

"Now, let's start from the top," he said as he picked up his number one song sheet for the show, "You Are the Sunshine of My Life." He had been using this song because the words conveyed a message he wanted to give his audience. "They" were the sunshine in his life, had been, and always would be. The lyrics and the tune conveyed the right message to get him started.

"You Go to My Head." Song number two. "Now, how long have I been singin' this? And this was arranged by Nelson. Listen to the words. 'And I find you spinnin' round in my brain like the bubbles in a glass of champagne.' Now how many broads and guys out there have gone through the same shit? They meet somebody, they go out once or twice, then they can't wait to see each other again and again and again, still I say to myself, 'get a hold of yourself. Can't you see that it never can be?' It's when they doubt that someone can love them, that someone can care for them. Then they go on to say, 'I'm certain that this heart of mine hasn't a ghost of a chance in this crazy romance. You go to my head.'

"How da hell do you write these kinds of words? Put 'em to music? How da hell do you do that?" He slowly shook his head from side to side. He had been through romances like this, but never could put them into music. He had lived the romance, which had put scars on his soul. Now that was his gift, to make the music and words come out of him as a living tribute to broken romances.

As he sat there at the piano, he reminisced about the loves in his life. Nancy, Ava, and others that had slipped through his fingers. Juliet Prowse, Lauren Bacall, and some that he had forgotten. "Can't you see that it never can be?" jumped out at him from the song in front of him.

"Can't you see that it never can be?" he whispered to himself as he felt this glow and warmth come all over his body.

"Too many memories. Too many lonely nights." He continued as his mind traveled back and forth over all the years and over all the pain that these songs and he had been through. "You go to my head," he breathed.

Chapter Six
A Preview

There he was in a pool of blood screaming his fool head off. He was just about to leave his mother's womb, but his head was in the wrong position. They had to pull him out with forceps. A botched up birth. The midwife screwed it all up. She panicked. Thank God for his grandmother. She grabbed the forceps and somehow managed to grab Frank by the head and neck and ear and pulled him out. He was a big baby. Fourteen pounds. He came out screaming, clinging, and kicking for life, grasping for air. He would be scarred for life.

In 75 years nothing had changed. This was to be a preview of his whole life, clinging, kicking, and screaming for his right to be Number One.

Did he actually remember this? Or had the story been told so many times that his birth story had been embedded in him? The left side of his neck was scarred pretty badly, and the bottom of his left ear was almost cut off, but here he was ready to meet the world on December 12, 1915. Growing up, he would get into lots of fights because of that neck and ear. Kids were cruel, and somebody would always pick him out of a crowd and scream at him that he had a chicken neck. A no-good "Guinea Chicken Neck." He became a loner. He had a few friends he could trust, but most of the time he was alone. Even at home, his parents and relatives talked about his neck. "What a shame. He's such a good-lookin' boy, but his neck and his ear. That's too bad."

As far as he was concerned the scar was a curse. Why me? Many times growing up he thought he was probably better off dead. He never grew up with any one friend. He became a loner. He never really became a close friend with anyone, perhaps Dean, but that was too many years later.

Frank snapped out of this reverie and calmly crossed his arms and slowly began to sink into his chair. He tried to come back to the present, but his mind would not let him go. His mind brought him back to his boyhood dreams and aspirations.

His bedroom was his castle, his domain. After a fight with some punky kid or his mother's tirade against him, he would find refuge in his room. Here he could be himself. Here he could dream.

As long as he could remember he wanted out. His mother was always on his back, and the old man, shit, he always sided with her. Frank always was "a good son." He didn't argue back or get into trouble with other kids, and somewhere he had learned to respect his parents, and all his life he did that. In his own way he loved them and they loved him.

In his bedroom is when he dreamed of becoming a singer.

Habits start at a young age, and some never leave you. Being alone and nearly dying changes you. Having nobody to talk to changes you. Being a boy changes you. But being alone to fend for yourself—that really changes you, and you don't even know why or when that happens. You grow up in your own thoughts, in your own world. All your dreams are yours to live with in your own head, to fight with, to take you away from the life you live into another world, the world of fantasy. And if you have the "balls" or the "moxie" or the "guts" and the talent, dreams happen. This takes work, lots of work, but dreams happen. Dreams don't come overnight, but they happen.

Life happens, and you have to hang on real tight. You cannot let anyone in. You have to make all the decisions. You are alone. They left him alone. Oh, sure, they fed him and bought his clothing, but alone, always alone in his head, trying to figure life out for himself. Who can he talk to? Who understands him anyway? Who gives a shit? The old man? Hell, he can't even talk for himself, and mom runs shotgun over everybody.

Alone! Alone! Alone! This became his way of life. An engineer? What the hell did she know? Wanting to be Crosby was all he ever wanted to happen. Frank had his room where he could dream, where he could act out exactly how the dream would happen. The dream probably happened later than he thought, yet his dream, his lifetime dream, came true.

He could visualize himself on the stage singing with applause after applause demanding that he continue. All kinds of movie offers coming in and becoming the number-one star in Hollywood. The dream was always the same: Frank on top of the world becoming the number-one entertainer. Always the same dream, and he ate, slept, and drank that dream every day, every day.

He became Crosby, and more.

He did not exactly remember when he wanted to become a singer, but somewhere in his teen years the dream began to develop. As a little boy he began to sing. His parents thought he was so cute singing that way. Radio was the big thing then, and they had a radio. Most of the time the station was set on some Italian station where his parents and relatives would listen to native Italian music and, naturally, Italian opera. Caruso, Gigli, the big Italian stars were opera singers.

He was even encouraged to sing opera, but that wasn't the voice he had. He had a small voice, and that music was not for him. Not opera. He knew all about opera from the old folks, and later on when he met John Quinlan he began to really appreciate and love the music. Yet as a teenager, that music was for highbrows. He began to listen to the music of his day, jazz. Soft jazz, loud jazz, swing music. He loved jazz, and somewhere in his mind, thoughts of singing came out.

He could listen to Rudy Valle, Russ Columbo, and Bing Crosby. Bing became his idol. All these guys sang with the big bands, and as far as Frank was concerned, he was hooked.

School was out. He never enjoyed going. Years later he regretted that, but you can't go back. Music, singing—that was what he was all about.

The singing dream probably got into his head when he was just a kid. He began singing for his parents and relatives, and naturally, they praised him to the heavens. And every once in a while one of the uncles would give a penny or two, and if he got a nickel he was in heaven.

When his father had the saloon, he would be asked to sing once in a while when he was helping out cleaning, sweeping, something. Now there he made "the big money," sometimes as much as twenty-five cents—a whole quarter!

Sometimes his friends would get together on the street corner or at parties and they would sing together as a quartet. Frank was always part of that. He had a good voice. He could hold a tune and always wanted in, wanted to be part of a singing group.

Frank tried to remember when the decision came that he wanted to be like Bing Crosby. But for the life of him he never could remember. Whenever and however that decision came, nobody, but nobody, could dissuade him. His parents tried. He even tried not singing. Hell! He needed the money. At 17 he was already singing in saloons and local clubs. To make the big time took time and patience. Frank had the time but never the patience.

When Frank quit his "real" job, his father finally threw him out of the house. Frank got jobs here and there, and then he began to take singing lessons. The music never left him. The arguments between him and his parents never subsided. His mother finally gave in and bought him an amplifier and microphone. His father never gave in. His father never thought the music would last.

There was the rub—his father!

You want pain! Suck on that one for a while. Your old man doesn't even believe in you. Do I believe in my son? Frank thought, *Have I encouraged him?* That thought just rolled around in Frank's head for a while as he tried to think if his relationship with Frank Jr. was any different than the one that he had with his father. *I may have been better than my old man, but what about me and Frank Jr.?*

That thought about him and Frank Jr. always seemed to raise itself. To roam around and around in his head. He never could find a solution that satisfied him. He tried his best. Sometimes Frank thought that his lifestyle made a good relationship almost impossible.

He unfolded his arms and turned himself around to look out the window and think about what could have been and what should have been. Slowly he turned, faced the piano, and with moistened eyes, he picked up "The Show" again and began to review.

"'Night and Day,' Cole Porter. Now this one has been with me from the beginning." As he reached back into time, he remembered that this was one of the songs that propelled him into the headlines. He first sang "Night and Day" with Tommy Dorsey, and when he went solo, he sang the same song to boost his entrance into the entertainment field. "This guy could write music. He was queer, but he could put music together. Always a little bouncy. Always a lot of pain. If I remember right, he supposedly wrote, 'I Get a Kick Out of You' after being beaten up by a truck driver for makin' a pass at him. But shit, he really could do music.

"Seems all these tunes I sing are sad and melancholy. I tell ya, they were written for me. I'm just a lucky bastard."

As he opened the song sheet and faced the keys to the piano he began to plunk on the keys, and then something strange happened. He became the music and the lyrics. He could not help himself. This feeling came over him like a metamorphosis. It always happened. The change came quickly beginning from his head down to his toes. As soon as the music began and he raised his head to sing, he would be transformed into the music. He became the person jilted, he became the one longing for the other, and he became the one waiting . . . waiting for the other. He became the music, the poetry personified in the lyrics.

"Like the beat, beat, beat of the tom-tom," he whispered and softly hit the proper keys.

"When the jungle shadows fall.

"Like the tick, tick, tock of the stately clock," he whispered again, enunciating the word correctly hitting the "T" softly with the tongue, the "K" bouncing gently off his palate, and his teeth placed in such a way that the "ticktock" of his voice sounded like the clock on the wall. All the words pronounced correctly, and each letter given the proper sound.

The Jersey accent was gone—*dese* and *dose* disappeared. *Repeatin'* became *repeating,* beat, beat became the tom-tom. The transformation was remarkable and immediate, happening every time the music began.

"Night and day, you are the one, Only you beneath the moon or under the sun, Whether near to me, or far, It's no matter, darling, where you are I think of you, Day and night, night and day, why is it so?"

"What happens to a guy to write dis kinda music? To put dese lyrics to the music? He's gotta be hurtin'; he's been slammed against the wall; he's been beat up by some broad. My God, he's been through hell and back."

As he said this he pushed himself off the piano stool and just stood there gazing at nothing in particular.

Frank knew he'd been there!

"I remember when I lost my voice. Things weren't goin' too good. It was all goin' downhill, and then the voice went. I was at the Copa. Talk about being beat up. I did a bunch of prayin' then. And lots of sleepless nights. I used to walk alone through the streets of New York. In my head I'd hear, 'It's over! It's over! It's over!' And I'd cry out against it, 'No! No! No!' Those were terrible days. A lot of booze. A lot of cryin'. A lot of walkin'. And alone. All alone. Who the hell was I gonna talk to about it? Ya think anybody cared? The old man always said it wouldn't last. My mother, shit, she was too filled with herself and her political cronies. Nancy, she was too good for me."

As he spoke Nancy's name his voice softened and as he glanced into the distance, he began to picture her. He shook his head slowly in approval as he thought of her.

"Alone! Alone! Even the guys around me all they wanted from me was for me to sing so they could make some money off of me." Frank was always alone. Even with people around him, he was alone. He had built that persona that made him that way. His attitude—"Don't tell me what to do," was legend. Oh, he could be suggested to. He probably could count on the fingers of one hand the number of people he really trusted.

Frank had been a loner and would die one. When you have been brought up all your life that you can only count on yourself for anything, you build a wall around yourself. You don't let too many people in. Those you let in only get to see a little bit of the real person. You are too afraid to let your emotions all hang out there. Frank trusted only himself, and he never let anybody in to see the real Sinatra.

Being Sinatra was not easy, yet Frank had been able to mold the man. He had been able to take some words and some music, two-and-one-half to three-and-one-half minutes and make people cry or laugh and get so emotionally involved that they were the ones who were crying out—

"Under the hide of me, There's an oh such a hungry yearning burning inside of me, And this torment won't be through, Until you let me spend my life making love to you, Day and night, night and day."

They became the song and the lyrics. He had captured them! He had brought them into his world! He was able to lay his heart and soul out for them to absorb, for them to feed on, for them to cry on.

What a gift he was given! Pure gift!

And the world was his audience.

He crossed his arms again, slowly sat on the piano stool, looked at the music sheet in front of him, and whispered, "In the silence of my lonely room, I think of you. Day and night, night and day."

He breathed in and out slowly as he wandered down memory lane, and then strolled back to the present, the Show.

"'Soliloquy.' They could have put that further down into the program. Maybe number 7 or 8, but it's okay where it is. Now that's great music. I always wanted to do that movie, but they gave it to Gordon McRae. I would have been perfect for the part. A barker and real hustler. That's me all the way. I've been a hustler all my life." He smiled. He remembered hustling from one job to another, singing wherever he could. It was he and his microphone. He had even agreed to sing with the Hoboken Four, and they won the Major Bowes amateur show. He had the opportunity to travel the country and sing. He probably had been to every joint in the Hoboken area. He even did a few stints on radio. No real money, but it kept him alive, alive with the thoughts of greater things to come. And, always alone! Alone! Alone!

Yes, there was Nancy, and she was the only one encouraging him, saying he could do it. Nancy was always there listening to his dreams, his desires. She was the only one who kept building him up, who kept telling him he could make the big time. Yet even with her, he was alone; going for auditions, being turned down; singing and no applause. He never said he could not make the big time. He never got down on himself. There was a spirit in him that kept the drive going, that kept that light shining, a spirit that only the great ones know about, and yet they cannot explain the reason. The spirit is there, and they are grateful, and they keep going. They never stop until they reach the peak of their profession. That's what happened to Frank. Frank had that spirit which stayed with him all his life.

"Sometimes I wondered if I could have that big voice like Luciano and sing those arias like he does."

Frank had acquired a love for "highbrow" music as a kid. The radios or phonographs in the homes and stores in his Italian neighborhood always had opera. That music was part of their heritage and who they were. The opera music kept them attached to their roots. When Frank took lessons with Mr. Quinlan, he always spoke about the great Italian tenors and the great Italian operas.

"To project, to feel the music, listen to the great ones. They feel it here. And here and here," Mr. Quinlan would shout out as he touched his head, his heart, and his gut. "That's where the music has to come from. It's not just a bunch of words that somebody throws together. The music writer and the lyrics have to go together. These writers experienced those emotions. They have lived those thoughts.

"You! You! You, have to interpret that. You have to find it inside yourself to tell your audience what they have written. You are the interpreter; always; always remember this is your music! Yours. Nobody else's but yours! Only yours!" If he told Frank that once, he told him one hundred times. Frank learned the lesson well. There weren't many, but he learned well. Frank not only learned well, he also lived that emotional roller coaster.

Frank fell in love with the music of Puccini. He even connected with the man. They had many things in common. Puccini was a great artist, a wonderful composer, a ladies' man, and a man about town. Frank often thought they came from the same mold.

Frank became passionate about Puccini and his music. He loved *La Bohème,* and when Luciano sang "Che gelida manina," Frank would listen in awe and tears would form, the emotion was so great. The music would wrap itself around Frank, and Frank would be lifted to another place, a place where he would be smothered with love, a place that took away all the cares and anxieties of this world, a place of bliss and happiness. As the music wrapped itself around him, he thought that this is what heaven was like.

"I wonder what it would have been like to have a voice like Pavarotti. That would have been a gas, but like Nancy Jr. said, 'Then who would have been Sinatra?' Each to his own. Each to his own," he explained to an empty room.

"Where the hell did I see that picture of Puccini, a statue, somewhere in Italy, and he's got a cigarette in his hand? Shit! Imagine that, a cigarette in his hand. He even beat Smokey." He laughed as that thought rolled around in his head.

Then he bowed his head as the memories of Sammy came tumbling out. Frank had been very instrumental in Sammy's life. Telling him to stop dancing and start singing. And when Sam lost his eye, Frank had been the one paying the bills and being the psychiatrist to get him back on his feet and back on stage. "Now there was a talent." Frank breathed the words out softly as not to disturb the memory.

As Frank began to review the words to "Soliloquy," his eyes glanced at the next song on the program, "You Will Be My Music." "Now there's a guy who tried to set the record straight. Good ole Joe! Joe Rapaso." Frank detested today's music, "Rock 'n' roll they call it. They should be throwin' rocks at it and rollin' that crap off the highest building they could find. Who the hell ever came up with that kind of drivel? And they all have to swing their ass to get attention. Shit, they can't sing. They just scream out words and yell the music. How the hell can you compare it to our music, dis music?" he yelled, as he shook the work sheets in his hand.

Frank had contempt for today's music, especially the gyrations of Elvis Presley. Elvis was doing what Frank was doing 50 years ago. He had the young girls swoonin'. They both had great managers.

"What the hell does he do?" he whispered angrily. "Shakes his hips like he's gettin' laid on stage. Screams some crap out and the girls go bonkers. They all wanna get laid by him. And they call it music. It's crap. That's what it is.

"Joe Raposo, you did the right thing when you put it down on music. It won't sell, but we needed to hear it. We needed to be told that good music never dies and the people out dere make the music, and they make us," he thought as his mind went over the thousands and thousands of people he had sung for. He loved them all!

"George and Ira Gershwin," he said as he picked up "They Can't Take That Away from Me." "Now they could write music, and their rhythm was somethin' else. It was the easiest music to put strings to."

Frank loved to have "strings," violins, in his music. He had listened well to Mr. Quinlan, and the strings came from the classical music of Heifetz and Brahms. Frank had a love for Brahms, and he always insisted that Tommy Dorsey add a few strings to his orchestra. They went through a few rumbles on that issue. Tommy was tight with a dollar, but he also had the talent to know that strings gave the band another dimension, and with Frank's voice, it was the perfect fit. If Tommy had two violins, Frank would ask for four. Frank was always trying to persuade Tommy for more strings. When Frank went on his own, and especially when Nelson became his arranger, the strings and the voice of Sinatra were all that was needed to make beautiful music.

"The way you wear your hat, The way you sip your tea, The memory of all that, No, they can't take that away from me."

He slowly spoke the words and one-handed the piano. "Now why did I screw up last night?" He again went back to last night's performance. "I know dese words and the music inside and out—backward and forward. It's gotta be the pills. Shit! Don't get old! Grandma used to tell me dat. Don't get old she'd say. 'You know, Frankie, when I put my feet on the floor in the morning, when I get up, I pray that God gets me through today. That's right. One day at a time.' Every time she'd drop somethin' or forget somethin' she'd say, 'Don't get old, Frankie. It's no good.' Grandma was right. Don't get old! And, don't take those damn pills!"

"New York! New York!" was next. Frank had a habit, a good one, of telling his audience and giving credit to the people who wrote the music and lyrics and to the one who arranged the music. He truly believed that all these songwriters were responsible for his career. His job was to interpret the music and lyrics. He always felt he could do this because in most cases he had been there and done that. He was singing about himself. He owed those guys and always gave them credit. Frank found this the best way of saying thank you, his way of being noble and kind.

"Last night," he yelled, "I couldn't remember that Don had arranged the music; Frank Jr. had to give it to me as I fumbled around in my head tryin' to think of it. I couldn't even remember Don Costa. What kind a shit am I pullin'?" This whole happening saddened Frank. He had thought of letting go. He was 75. *When do I stop?* He thought. "When am I gonna call it quits? I tried it once but I was too young then. I couldn't sit still. I had to get out. Bein' home all the time it wasn't for me. Shit, if I keep doin' what I did last night"—he paused with the sentence in midair. Frank knew if he kept that up he would have to go. He did not want to embarrass himself, and he definitely did not want to let his audience down.

The thought of letting go and quitting flashed through him again and he shuddered instinctively. "The last time was how long ago, 10, 15 years?"

He had thought to go out while he was still on top.

"What a shit head I was. That was a stupid move. That was da worse decision I ever made. Da worse!"

As these thoughts of retirement raced through his head again he began to feel uneasy. He started to rise from the stool but stopped and slowly lowered himself back down again. His mind went blank for a few moments as this awful situation of retiring and memory loss coursed through his mind and body.

His hands began to tremble a little as he caught himself and grasped the top of the piano with both hands, and with every ounce of energy in his body he screamed at the top of his lungs, "NO! NO! NO!" and jumped off the stool.

"I want to go out on top just like a ball player. Ya gotta leave when you're on top of your game. Don't stay for another year and another year—this hurts, that hurts. No, Frankie boy, leave on top. And if I'm going to go, then I want to die on the stage. God, if you're gonna take me, then let me go on the stage; don't let me whimper out like a baby. Not me! Not me! I can't go out like that. Not like that," he bellowed.

And as he spit out these last words his mind, as minds do, flashed to an old friend, Joe DiMaggio. "Last time up at bat—a home run, but Dimag', that no good WOP; he stayed too long."

Frank remembered the good days when he and Joe hung out together. Drinking buddies. Frank had even helped Joe in that fiasco, playing detective against Marilyn.

"Now that was a real fiasco. We had the wrong room. Wrong buildin'. Good thing we got outta there. And then the son of a bitch accuses me of tryin' to steal Marilyn away from him."

"Man, we had some argument. I was ready to take a bat to da bum. Man, was he jealous. He probably didn't let her go to the bathroom without followin' her around.

"The poor bastard. He spent his life lookin' after her, and then when she croaks on those pills, he wouldn't even let me come to the funeral. He should fry in hell," he screamed as he banged his hand on the piano keys and the sound cascaded all over the room.

"Who the hell would want her? She was a sloppy broad, but, man, what a looker. She had a way of walkin' and lookin' at ya that could knock your socks off. She wasn't bad in bed either," and as he smiled he thought about those days with her. "But, man, was she sloppy. She had too much stuff goin' on in her life. She wouldn't get off dose fuckin' pills; that's what killed her, dose fuckin' pills."

As he said this he jumped back to the present, frowned, and whispered, "I can go out on top, get rid of dese fuckin' pills, do a little more rehearsin', ya know; you're not gettin' any younga'," he said emphatically and smiled.

Frank came back to reality when the pills came to mind. "I know it's those fuckin' pills. No more of that shit! And no more talk of retirin'." He exploded as he stacked the music sheets together and looked for the next song on the program.

His body calm now, he quickly became the musician, the lover of song, the interpreter of the lyric as he softly began to speak, "I've got you under my skin, I've got you deep in the heart of me, So deep in my heart that you're really a part of me, I've got you under my skin. I've tried so not to give in, I said to myself: this affair never will go so well."

"Now dere's a great song. Who da hell wrote that? Yea! Cole Porter! He always had a way with music. Man, he was good. His music always had a lift to it. It kinda grabs ya in the head, and then bounces right down to your gut. Makes you, and the broad that you're singin' about, wanna get together, wanna make it so bad they can't wait to see each other and grab each other and make love to each other.

"He's got that clip in his rhymes so that ya can't wait for the next line and the next one."

"I'd sacrifice anything come what might, For the sake of havin' you near, In spite of a warnin' voice that comes in the night, And repeats, repeats in my ear."

"Ya see, dere it is—dere it is," he exclaimed with excitement as if this were the first time he had seen or read those words.

And as far as Frank was concerned this was always the first time. He had the uncanny ability of being able to view the music and words as if they were the first time he viewed them because he had this wonderful admiration for his audience and a brilliant interpretation of the words and music, and this great respect for the writer, lyricist, and arranger of the song.

Yet somehow, he was able to put these strands together and let everything become his music.

As far as he was concerned, they *were* listening to him for the first time and he had to give them his best. There he was alone on the stage singing one on one. For Frank, that moment was always the first time. As far as he was concerned, he would rather they turn up the house lights and then he could look in their eyes and make love to each one of them.

He once said, "I get an audience involved, personally involved, in a song because I'm involved myself. It's not something I do deliberately. I can't help myself."

"Yes, I've got you under my skin."

This was a tune that he always sang about his audience. This was a love song that explained his relationship with the audience. They were under his skin. He would sacrifice anything for the sake of having them near. Just the thought of them makes him stop 'cause he's got them under his skin. And when the music interlude chimes in, he could feel that whole audience inside of him and all over him. Yes, that's where they belonged: "under his skin!"

As he finished the next-to-the-last number from the show he was beginning to feel a little better about himself, and that brought on that charm of a smile that had thrilled millions.

The thought of giving up the pills or at least cutting back improved his whole look on things. He knew he could not give them all up, but he was going to talk to Barbara and the doctor to see what could be done.

"Ahh! 'One for My Baby.' That's always a keeper. Great lyrics. Johnny Mercer was good with lyrics."

"It's a quarter to three, there's no one in the place, Except you and me. So set 'em up, Joe, I got a little story, I think you should know, We're drinking, my friend, to the end, Of a brief episode, Make it one for my baby, And one more for the road."

"Man, how many times have I been there? Talk about livin' the music, man, this is one of dose." He spoke as he looked deeply into the music sheet.

He was mesmerized by the words as his mind traveled over all the times he had spent at a bar just shootin' the breeze. Just drinking, putting nickels in the jukebox, and listening. That's how he had met Jilly. Jilly had a bar, not much of a place, on the west side of NYC near the theater district. Frank would wind up there when he first started singing in New York. This bar was the right atmosphere for him. He could talk to Jilly, get a bite to eat, have a few drinks, and unwind. Always at 3:00 or 4:00 in the morning and stay a few hours. He would close the place with Jilly. They became good friends.

What really sealed the friendship was when Frank was just starting out. He had gone there for his usual nightcap when some guys walked in and recognized Frank, and they began to razz him, and then after a couple of drinks, started talking about beating up "the pussy." Scary stuff and Frank was cornered.

Well, he didn't have to worry. Jilly came walking around the bar with a baseball bat in his hand, and even though these guys were bigger than him, he told them in no uncertain terms to get out or he would wipe them off the face of the earth. "Knock da shit out of dem," that's what he said. Well, that cemented the relationship, and Jilly has been with Frank ever since.

"Now Frank Jr. could have ended with 'Angel Eyes.' Those are good finale numbers," he said matter-of-factly. He was now getting his composure back. He was almost ready to go on stage. It was not showtime, but his mind was ready. He was feeling better.

"Now, where the hell is 'Angel Eyes'? I know it's around here someplace. I just talked about it." He got up and walked over to a bookcase that had more song sheets than books.

"It's gotta be on top," he spoke calmly to himself.

"Ah, there we go," he said as he reached for the top music sheet on the third shelf, "Angel Eyes."

In the excitement of seeing the music sheet he wanted and in the place he expected, his fingers awkwardly pulled out several sheets of music, with most of them falling to the floor.

"Shit!" he exploded. "What a stupid ass." He quickly bent down to pick up the music sheets. They had scattered all over the floor.

"Son of a bitch," he said. "Look at this crap." As he gathered them together, he picked one up, turned the song sheet around, and there to his amazement was: "I'm a Fool to Want You."

Chapter Seven

Ava–The Beginning

As he stared at the song sheet and the words shouted out to him, his mind traveled back 30 or 40 years. He remembered how she had left the very last time they tried to make their love affair work.

Frank looked at the song sheet again and remembered that Ava had died in January of this year.

She had died. The love affair over! Finally over!

He wanted to scream and yell but could not. He could hardly breathe. He opened his mouth, and nothing came out. He could feel his chest grasping for air. Although the house was well ventilated, he was gasping.

"It's over. It's over," he kept repeating in his mind. He clasped his hands on his chest, ripping the shirt away from his body, trying to open the cavity so more air could go in and give more room for his heart. His heart was getting ready to explode. The pounding was unbearable.

He began to shake as he slowly collapsed to the floor, first to his knees, and then having no strength whatsoever, his limp body slid just like a wet rag and he lay there. Then he began to cry. His face buried in his arms. Tears began to roll down his face, and then straight onto the floor. He was shaking all over and could not stop even if he wanted to. His breath came in short gasps. He banged his hands on the floor until they screamed with pain.

At the same time the wailing began, the loud cries coming from the pit of his stomach, the loud anguish, and the heart-rending cry that began from the depth of his stomach and exploded from his mouth and vibrated throughout the room. This was the moaning and wailing of someone who had lost a loved one in a struggle between life and death. Frank had lost, death had won. In his mind she was still alive, but nowhere would he be able to hold her, caress her, or talk to her in the way that lovers do: in a smile, a glance, a touch. The love affair was over.

He was filled with despair, and his sobbing and cries filled the room. After several minutes he sat up on the floor, the tears had stopped, his erratic heartbeats had subsided, and most of the trembling had gone. Every once in a while a large sob came out of nowhere and the trembling would begin again.

He tried to hate her but couldn't. He had loved her with a passion that no one could or would understand. She had broken him many times before, but this time was final.

"It's over," he said sadly. His life would be changed forever. His soul had been touched and broken and the pain of this torrid love affair would remain with him forever—until the day he died.

From the day he met her, Frank would bring Ava wherever he went. She would remain part of him. She was inside of him for the entire world to see. You see, Frank was a saloon singer and as he was that, he also became the person in the music, in the lyrics. He had been broken and could sing about those love affairs. Frank had loved and could croon about it. Frank had been there, and the music that was given to him was all about that. Every time that a ballad was open for him to sing, he would open himself to the world, live, and despair in all the lyrics.

Mr. Quinlan had been right! You had to feel the music. You had to live the lyrics. You are the heart of the music. As he raised himself off the floor, straightened up, and brushed the wetness from his face and adjusted his clothing he wanted to call somebody, but who? Dino? Sammy? Maybe Nancy Jr.? Ava?

"No! No! Nobody can help," he screamed out.

As he thought of more names to call he began to realize that he could only get out of this by himself.

This had always been the way—Frank, alone, against the world. He had fought the establishment, and he won. Alone! Always alone!

As his mind slowly returned to the present and his bodily movements began to settle down, he straightened up and walked over to the stereo, found the CD of *La Bohème,* placed the disc into the recording system, and began to listen to the love affair of Mimi and Rudolfo. As the music engulfed him he began to cry. This time for the loss of a loved one. The quiet sobbing, the chest heaving. The tears are all about death.

The death of love in his life.

The death of unrequited love.

He had always known that the love he gave her was not given back. Ava wanted to love desperately, but her love only came on her terms. Many people, especially women, idolized Frank, and Ava was jealous. To tell the truth, they were both jealous.

They came from the same mold. They both wanted and needed love desperately. They never received love from their parents. Sex was the only thing that satisfied them both. When they met, their sex was a collision of neediness. They needed each other, and they needed independence.

He was willing to give up some of his for her, but she wasn't willing to do that. She needed to be free. A lithe spirit. She tried. He tried. The affair didn't work. The affair never would. And now . . .

As he picked up the song sheet, "I'm a Fool to Want You," his body began to sink to the floor. He collapsed on his knees, his back and head hunched over them as his arms wrapped themselves over his head. He began to shake.

"It's over. It's over," he sighed again as he began to moan and sob.

"She's gone. She's gone," he cried out quietly but in a voice that went through him as he continued to shake.

He remembered her death in January of this year as the tears and sobs took over his whole body. He began to shudder uncontrollably. He knew he had lost his love. The love of his life. He knew that he would never hear her voice again. Never be able to see her again. Never be able to touch her again. Death is final and comes quickly without a sound and takes away.

"Sometimes I wonder if she ever existed. Was she real or some figment of my imagination? I can never see her again," he whispered through tears and a voice that was almost nonexistent.

Slowly as he uncurled himself from a fetal position, he crawled on all fours to the nearest wall a few feet away, turned, and sat on the floor with his back propped against the wall. He was now sobbing, with tears flowing gently down his face. His face was drained of its color as he sat there thinking, thinking, thinking.

"Why didn't I go to see her? Shit, I knew she was sick. I knew she was dying. Why didn't I go?" He shouted out those last words as the sobs began to rack his body, as the voice of Rodolfo in *La Bohème* echoed in the background.

Last year Frank had spoken to Carmen, her maid, from time to time and even sent money to pay expenses but had never spoken to Ava. Frank had been busy with tours that year, but now he wondered aloud why he had not taken the time to visit.

He had always gone. Every time she cried out, every time she needed him, he dropped everything and ran to her. Her problems were his problems. Her life was his life. She became part of him, whether she needed money, advice, or just someone to talk to—she called; he was there.

Everyone knew. They were still in love with each other. They could not live together. Ava knew, but Frank could never understand. He only went along with her wishes.

In all probability, his stubbornness had kept him away. Maybe because he was married to Barbara, or maybe there were too many obligations. But as he thought about the reasons for not going he realized that they were all lame excuses. He should have gone! He still loved her!

"Why? Why? Why? Why didn't I go?" he berated himself.

Slowly, he got on all fours again and began to crawl back to the pile of song sheets that had fallen from the piano and there on top he picked up, "I'm a Fool to Want You."

He slowly turned and squatted there among the song sheets and began to read the words that had haunted him for the last 40-some odd years.

"I'm a fool to want you, I'm a fool to want you, To want a

love that can't be true, A love that's there for others too, I'm a fool to hold you, Such a fool to hold you, To seek a kiss not mine alone, To share a kiss that devil has known, Time and time again I said I'd leave you, Time and time again I went away, But then would come the time when I would need you, And once again these words I had to say, Take me back, I love you, Pity me, I need you, I know its wrong, it must be wrong, But right or wrong I can't get along Without you."

"How the hell did I ever write this song?" he screamed.

"How the hell did I ever sing it?" he moaned.

"When was the last time I saw her?" he whispered as he tried to go back in time to picture that last time he saw her, but could not place anything in his mind at this present time. He began to sob again, quietly.

"It's over, it's over," he said in desperation.

His mind raced back in time when he had first met her. She had been with Mickey Rooney, her husband at that time, and his first words to her were about marrying her if Mickey had not seen her first.

She was simply gorgeous. A body that was to "kill for," green eyes that could turn him over and over. The way she used those eyes when looking at him. They enticed him; they engulfed him. There were times that when she looked at him he would have given her his soul, and there were times during that torrid relationship that he had done so.

"Pity me, I need you," he said slowly. "What a way to love, that I needed pity. And in those days, I really needed her so badly, and I wanted her to pity me and take me back. I would call and call. She would answer. When she would say no, I would go off into drunken binges, sometimes screamin' and yellin', really makin' a jerk out of myself. And da last time I almost killed myself," he said desperately.

"And sometimes she would have pity on me and take me back, and then I was on a cloud, takin' the first plane or train to get me to where she was. I would literally drop everything when she said, 'Yes, let's try again.'

"We would get together and there was nothin' like it. I think I would go back to her now if she called, because for me and for her it was as if it was our first meeting, our first lovemaking. It was as if the world was just beginning and we were Adam and Eve, all alone without a care, only a desire for the sight of each other and the touch and feel of each other. It was an explosion of the cosmos."

He remembered one evening when they had stolen away to her apartment and she was in a particularly romantic mood. As they lay on the bed, she bent low over Frank's back to lay her cheek on his shoulder. She seemed to need him, and this alone started his pulse pounding as he could feel the blood flow through his veins.

"Frank," she moaned as she moved her mouth to his ear, her tongue tracing and slipping inside to arouse him to wakefulness. He began to groan, and his heart began to pound furiously. With her teeth she pulled and tugged on his earlobe, then moved to experiment with his neck and down his chest.

"I want you," she murmured. Quickly she began to take her lips over him with the same thorough care as her tongue.

"My turn," he whispered. With nimble fingers, he loosened the tiny buttons down the front of her shirt. His lips followed, and she seemed to be ablaze as her newly exposed skin trembled under his hands and tongue. Ava seemed swept away, as through a hurricane of sensation as if caught in the eye of a storm. His hands cupped her upper thighs, his thumbs pressing insistently. Expertly, he unhooked her stockings, drawing them off slowly. Ava moaned, bending her leg around him to help him as torment and pleasure tangled.

For one heady moment his tongue lingered at the top of her thigh. His breath shot through the material into the core of her and left her moist and aching to come greedily back to his mouth. Ava gave kisses ardently, dragging Frank closer. Their bodies pounding and pulsing against each other with greater need. Frank never knew a passion so concentrated and volatile, while Ava struggled under him to find the ultimate release.

This was bliss! This was heaven! This was Frank and Ava!

"We would spend the first several hours talking, making love, talking, making love. The fury and passion was animal-like."

"Then as time went on and we began to talk, this picture would begin to crack. Sometimes it was me and sometimes it was her, but we had a way to make it happen. Unrequited love. We both wanted complete control. Neither one of us would give in; we were both very strong individuals. In this stupid fuckin' business you had to be or you couldn't survive. Whatever made us do it, we did it. The crack in the dream would begin and before you knew it we would be at each other, yellin', screamin', and even throwin' all kinds of shit at each other. Thank God we never hit each other. That would have been a disaster. This could last a day or two, or sometimes a week, and then it would be over. It would end with finality. It would end like death."

He paused momentarily, and then he slowly began to recite the words "and then would come the time when I would need her, and once again these words I had to say, 'take me back, I love you. Pity me, I need you.'"

"Pity me! Can you imagine me asking her for pity?" as he shook his head from side to side so very slowly. "But that's the way it was. I wanted her. I needed her. And ya know, I coulda' been happy just to have her pity," he said solemnly.

"Pity me, I need you" as he peeked at the song sheet again.

He paused for a moment, and then the crying began, almost like a whisper, with short gasps of air in between. Tears flowing steadily down a face that had been through many years of tragedies and many years of triumph. His shirt was damp as he grasped his chest, always trying to bring more air into his lungs.

He was dying inside.

Why couldn't they find the love in each other to have made the relationship work? Was this stupid business always in the way, the long hours, time spent away from home, the ego that you needed to survive in this business? Was that the reason?

Whatever the reason between them, they could not make their love affair work. They both tried several times, and disaster was always the outcome.

This thought of "trying" seemed to calm him. The pain seemed to ease as he continued this travelogue with Ava.

Whatever the reason, love for each other was a mess and would never and could never be reconciled.

Chapter 8
Unrequited Love

It was what it was, unrequited love.

As the crying subsided, he thought of a small town in California called India or Indigo or something Indian. They had shot up the town. They had made passionate love. What a night, a night never to be forgotten. A night full of hopes and dreams. A night that one could dream about. A night that happened and became surreal.

He had picked up Ava in his new convertible from some party. He had to coax her to come with him, twisting her arm, so to speak.

This was the beginning of their unrequited love affair.

He had been pursuing her for some time—stalking was a better way to describe his actions. He started very casually with walk-bys on movie sets. She was the new kid on the block, another starlet trying to make it in the movies. He had been there, but now he was on the rise, the big guy in town. His fall would come later. His fall never became a crash, only a spiraling descent, and then a meteoric rise that knew no bounds.

Frank smiled; that was another story, he thought.

When the attempts to date on the movie sets did not work he began to attend the parties that she attended, many times "just crashing the party" to talk to her.

His way with women was uncanny, yet Ava was always cool to him. Always polite, but cool. She kept her distance. The fact was that she really did not like him. He seemed to sense this, and her aloofness became the challenge. The challenge was to his manhood, and he acted accordingly.

Frank stopped and wondered if this was a challenge rather than falling in love. He had always admired good-looking women and had bedded down many of them. Was this the case with her, or was lust driving him? Did he really love her? Whatever the case, he knew in the finality of things he fell madly in love with her.

Ava had a way of talking and looking at him that aroused him, as he had never been aroused before. Her green eyes bore into him, and there was a kindness and gentleness to them as she smiled, and when she used that gutter language they were both famous for, his whole being was aroused, not only sexually but also mentally, wanting her to be part of his life.

Frank remembered when he was with her he could forget all of his problems. He immersed himself completely in her, her looks, her talk, her mind, and her outlook on life. Frank was in love.

Visiting her on movie sets, attending parties where he thought she might be. Always trying to pull her away, always trying to get her to say yes to his invitations. She always was rather cool and aloof to him. He could not understand why she was repelled by him. Could her aloofness be because he was married to Nancy? Marriage was considered sacred by everyone in those days. And the "other woman" was the vixen, getting the bad rap if the man left his wife for her. Most of the time the man pursued the woman, as in the case of Frank with Ava, but the woman was always guilty by association.

He had fallen for her as they say, "Hook, line, and sinker." She became his obsession.

And as he sat there his mind traveled back in time to that explosive night when all hell broke loose and this love affair of a lifetime began.

One night, the explosion took place.

He happened to come into a party and there she was, beautiful as ever. Actually, he did not just "happen" to come to this party; he always knew where she was. Well! Almost always. Through friends and acquaintances there were many parties going on and Ava, being the new kid on the block, was always invited, if only for publicity purposes. He was always on the lookout of where she was.

When he arrived, the same cat-and-mouse game began. He pursued, and she backed off. Well, this night he finally got to her. One thing led to another, and they left together in his new Cadillac convertible. On the way out, they grabbed two magnums of champagne and that crazy night began.

Frank smiled again as the years rolled back in his mind as he remembered the beginning of this one night, this explosion of a night.

They flew out of there because at this time they were both half in the bag. As soon as they left, with Frank driving, they headed toward the desert. No place in particular, just to be together, to have a few drinks and just let the night unfold.

He drove, they drank, they talked. And both of them were talkers. One always trying to outdo the other. They did not try to put each other down; the talking was only a means of getting attention. They both needed that special attention that neither had received as children. What a beautiful night for talking and driving.

He drove, they drank, they talked. Finally at some point on this desert road, Frank stopped the car. He just pulled over, no one in sight. The only light was from the stars that glistened and twinkled from a million miles away. And the moon was half full, yet looked whole and ripe for the picking. The desert was lit up with moonlight and stars.

Frank looked at Ava, turned off the engine and lights of the convertible, and crawled on to the backseat. He stood up on the seat and extended his hand to her. She looked at him, and then his hand, and after a few moments, she took his hand and crawled her way to the back of the car.

The lovemaking started slowly, the kissing, the caressing, and then the animal passion was aroused in both of them. They both began to "tear the clothes" off of each other and began to test the leather and the springs of this convertible. This was their first time together and was not to be their last, not even in this convertible.

This went on for about an hour, each one taking their turn of being the aggressor, not one of them giving in to the other. They both had met their match. They both knew their strengths, and they both enjoyed the exhilaration of being the leader and the follower. Leading and following was a first for both of them. This became lovemaking at its zenith, as if the gods had finally come through the cosmos and given their blessing to this copulation.

The lovemaking was also the first for the Cadillac.

Frank had made love to many women but never with such fury and such passion as Ava had for him. He was supposed to be the leader of this foray, but as soon as he got into the backseat he knew that he had met his match. She was as furious and as intense as he was. Their lovemaking was animal-like, with no boundaries. There was no one over the other. They were both equal in this pursuit of sexual eroticism.

Frank became aroused just thinking about that night and as the thought went through his head, he smiled and realized that the memory of that night could still awaken his feelings as he quietly said, "Not bad for 75."

Many times after this "Indio night," they were to talk to each other about that night. Why? Why? With such passionate lovemaking could they not find a way, some common ground, to make the love that they had for each other work in the real world? They had many "Indio nights" after that so why could they not make this love affair work as husband and wife? Why couldn't this passion be extended into the life of marriage that they both desperately wanted and needed for each other? There was no answer. They tried and failed.

Their relationship was a mystery to them and was to remain that way all their lives.

They both stepped out of the car, buck naked, and began to caress each other again. Then a strange thing happened. They looked at the sky at the same time and as they did this, a shooting star came into the horizon and whizzed by them. They quickly looked at each other, an omen, a portent of things to come.

Frank said slowly, "The gods are watching us." They reached for each other and kissed passionately. Before falling to the ground Frank remembered he had a blanket in the trunk of the car. He spread the blanket on the soft sand. They both entered onto this blanket of love and their lovemaking began again. The darkness around them made the stars shine ever so brightly. This time their lovemaking was slow, much more deliberate and with much more tenderness.

The aggressiveness of their first lovemaking had taken out that animal passion and now they were gentler with each other. With a sigh, Ava lay down on the blanket as Frank joined her. Softly and tenderly they caressed each other's body. They spoke in soft tones. Even the gutter words left them and only the cries of joy and quiet laughter filled the night air. Neither of them had ever experienced anything like this. The night was filled with words of joy, gladness, happiness, and even silence.

The need for Ava had crept up into Frank and grew stronger. Ava began to groan in anticipation as her heart began to pound as she sighed with desire, "I want you."

Frank reached for her as she gasped for air, anticipating what was to come. Before she could recover her breath his mouth was on hers. His tongue went deep in search of dark recesses as his weight pressed against her. Ava trembled as though a hurricane of sensation pulsed through her body, and she arched forward in complete submission of what was to come. Frank's hands moved all over her as she met him kiss for kiss. As she dragged him closer he began to pound and pulse against her.

In a half whisper Frank said, "You taste like no one else ever has."

There was an exotic cast in the moonlight and a sense of total abandonment as their naked bodies glowed with moisture under the desert stars.

Their passion built together until they came together as one body in ecstasy. Exhausted, they lay together in silence, spent. They were both aware that never before had either one ever experienced this kind of torrid lovemaking.

Upon completion of this lovemaking they raised themselves off the desert floor and looked each other over. They were both naked, and they automatically reached out their hands to one another as they slowly began to walk away from the car and proceed further into the desert. At first they walked, but then Frank began to pull a little harder on Ava's arm and they began to run deeper and deeper into the moonlit darkness, like two spirits frolicking in the night. They both stopped, breathing heavily, and both of them began to laugh loudly and scream at the top of their lungs.

They reached for each other, both spent from the torrid lovemaking and the dash into the desert, and kissed tenderly. They both expressed the love they had for each other and wanted all their nights to be like this one. They had found something special on this moonlit journey in the desert. They both thought this was the special other that they desired and needed.

They thought and tried, but this love affair was not to be.

They slowly returned back to the car helping each other brush the sand off their bodies. Then they both began to dress in the middle of this desert and the giggles began. They went on like this for about a half hour, finally putting their clothes on rather haphazardly and with no shoes, they grabbed the magnums, took a long hard drink, and resumed their journey, this time with Ava driving.

They both had forgotten the blanket.

As they were drinking and driving, Frank remembered that he had a thirty-eight with bullets in the glove compartment.

He had just received his permit to carry the gun from the Los Angeles police department.

Frank loaded the gun, raised himself, and sat on top of the front seat and began to shout cowboy style and shoot the gun off into the darkness and out into the desert. Naturally, Ava also joined in the whooping and yelling, swaying the car from side to side, both of them oblivious of the darkness and the recklessness of their ride.

They stopped several times to reload and Ava was given her turn with the gun. Frank drove, and she shot and shouted out into the darkness. Frank had purchased enough bullets to hold off a herd of buffalo.

They took aim at cactus or any other large object that they could see and when the headlights of the Cadillac caught something moving, they would literally go after the moving target with the car and with the gun, both taking turns trying to "kill the bastard."

This nonsense could have been the end of not only their careers but of their lives.

This is how they arrived in Indio; half dressed, wiped out, and "sixgun" in hand.

As they entered the town of Indio, they began to shoot up the town. Indio was one of those places where years ago they "rolled up the sidewalks at night." Frank and Ava had no idea where they were. One magnum of champagne was already left in the desert somewhere, and the effects of the second were beginning to leave them in no-man's-land, that place where reality does not exist anymore.

Store windows were shattered; some street lamps were actually hit and broken. Signs used as bull's-eyes were filled with holes. This was a scene from the Old Wild West when the cowboys rode in after a cattle drive, shooting up the town, looking for women and booze.

One store owner who lived above his store was accidentally shot at by Frank or Ava and almost killed. Fortunately for him, and for them, the bullet barely grazed the skin on his stomach. The incident probably would be a great story to tell his grandchildren, but upon happening I'm sure that the fear of death crossed this man's mind.

They had stopped the Cadillac in the middle of the street. Some lights had been turned on in the storeowner's second-floor rooms, with people poking their heads out of windows very carefully to see what the commotion was all about.

Someone called the sheriff.

The sheriff finally arrived and since they were out of bullets, he was able to "corral" them and place them both in jail.

The sheriff knew who Frank was, and wanting to help them out, he had Frank call his agent or lawyer. Frank immediately called Jack Keller, his agent, and explained the mess they were in. Jack was able to scrape together $30,000 in cash, rent a plane, and fly down to Indio and begin the process of bailing them out.

The sheriff, being either a nice guy or knowing he could make a few bucks for himself, decided to place both of them in the hotel room and wait for Jack to arrive and save the day for the two lovers and the town of Indio.

While Frank and Ava were waiting for Jack to arrive to "save the day," they were left in a hotel bedroom to cool off. The cooling off period ended in the same way that had started in the back of the Cadillac. When they were alone, they could not keep their hands and bodies off each other.

But this time exhaustion was beginning to take hold and their lovemaking was more subdued with more looking and smiling and less passion and talk. They finally fell asleep.

Within a few hours Jack arrived. With that $30,000 he was able to quiet the sheriff, the store owner who was slightly creased with the bullet, and restitution given to all the shopkeepers with broken store windows and signs with holes in them.

Jack Keller saved their careers. He came in on his white horse, just like in the movies, and chased the bad guys away.

This is how their love lives started and how this love affair would carry on in all the years they would know each other. Their lovemaking would always be torrid and passionate, one never giving in to the other. And their daily lives would be filled with the wild ride, shooting barbs at each other and doing all they could to scar each other with words or flying objects. And there was no Jack Keller on the "white horse" to save them.

Ava could survive without him—almost. Frank survived, but she never left his inner being. She was always there, not visible but always in the breath of a song, in the whisper of a word, in the sigh of a phrase. There she remained buried inside his being, inside his mind, but the pain, the passion, and the love that he had for her always came out in the song, in the ballads. He could not be rid of her; he was born to sing the ballads. This was his life's dream. He had to walk the walk.

Ava had captured him, and he could never let her go.

Frank now stirred a little from the floor as he reached over to the pile of fallen song sheets.

"How the hell was I supposed to forget her with songs like these?" he said softly as he picked up several song sheets. "I Hadn't Anyone Till You," "My Heart Stood Still," "The Very Thought of You," "It's a Lonesome Old Town," "Guess I'll Hang My Tears Out to Dry." "Shit, every time I stand in front of a mike and begin to sing she's in front of me, in back of me, above me. What did Quinny say about bel canto? Something about feeling the music, living in the words, being part of the song, being the heart of the song. I certainly live that!" he said emphatically, pronouncing every word and letter in that second language he was famous for.

"Even Nelson said if it wasn't for her I would have never become the singer that I was. She taught me to feel, to live the music, the hard way. Yet," he said remorsefully, "now she's gone." And the sobbing began again, and the tears, dripping from his eyes, began to splatter the song sheets on his lap. His chest was beginning to ache from all the crying and sobbing, so he began to rub his chest ever so slowly and started to gyrate his upper torso trying to get back to normal, trying to get back to the show, but his mind would not let him go, and so he backtracked again, letting himself be brought back to his near disaster.

Chapter Nine

The End?

He had left Columbia Records. Actually, they had let him go. That was the era in Frank's history where the end looked very close. Everything seemed to be shutting down on him. No movies, no recording dates, even the nightclubs were few and far between. If it wasn't for the "boyz," he would have been gone; even the voice was gone.

He even went back to the Paramount Theatre in 1952, only 7 years from his first big success, and sang to empty seats.

The dream was almost over, and that became very huge in Frank's life. He started to attend some sessions with a psychiatrist, but stopped as soon as he won the Academy Award.

What was not gone, and would never go, was this desire, this special drive inside of him that never let up, that never told him that "his dream" was over. He knew, somehow he knew, that his saturating desire to sing was not over and that somewhere, someplace, something was going to happen and he would be on top again. All his life that desire and drive would never let up.

Some have that desire and drive, and some don't. Frank had "it," whatever "it" was, and "it" was ingrained in his soul.

Frank's desire, or dream, began as a boy in Hoboken. He could not pin the exact date or time, but that desire began and never let up. Even today at 75 years of age, he had to go on the stage; he had to be up there. He really did not need the money or the accolades; he had already received two or three lifetime's worth. This insatiable desire was there from the beginning, and that never left him.

The desire would leave for a time, but then come back, sometimes pounding in his head. He had tried to retire a long time ago, but to no avail. He often thought what a "kick" if he dropped dead on stage singing, "It's quarter to three . . ." Just like Crosby did, die on the golf course, doing the thing you love most.

In the midst of all this pain and suffering, this perfect storm of anguish and despair, three things were stirring that were going to change the course of Frank's life and make him one of the biggest stars that Hollywood had ever seen.

Ava Gardner, *From Here to Eternity,* and that throat hemorrhage all helped to shape a career, stopped the career from collapsing, and put him on a meteoric rise that never ended until the day that Frank would die.

He would become that special icon of music and love, that special interpreter of word and music. He would make them forget the music, the composer, and the lyricist, and only remember the singer, the voice behind the microphone—Frank Sinatra—The Voice.

The hemorrhage, as the newspapers were told to call the throat incident, was a voice going downhill. The "hemorrhage" was a great publicity stunt. To tell the truth, the voice had simply given out. The voice had been strained both physically and mentally. The mental anguish of spiraling out of existence in the only thing that he ever wanted to do was too much for his body to take. Physically and mentally he was spent.

The voice gave out, and he almost collapsed from fright,

all while he was on the stage at the Copacabana in New York. He stepped on the stage to begin his show and nothing came out. Nothing. He left immediately and for the next few weeks received great medical attention. He had somehow strained his voice and was told to stop singing and even talking for the next few weeks. His career was spiraling down and in a few years he could have been just a memory, so the loss of a few shows was serious; yet, in the scheme of things, the loss of a few shows was nothing. He still had Ava, and all he needed was to rest his voice.

But something strange happened. When he began to sing again his voice had changed slightly. Prior to the "hemorrhage," his voice was light and soft, but after the throat healed, the voice became deeper and stronger. A much-richer timbre came out of his throat.

Listen to Frank before and after the throat incident. The voice changed and quite noticeably. This is the Sinatra we have grown to hear and love.

The movie *From Here to Eternity* was a stepping-stone to a comeback that Hollywood had never seen before. Many people had started, became stars, and within 10 years were gone. Not Frank!

He seemed to have had a connection to God, and that the music of Frank Sinatra would not be allowed to die. He had to be heard. He had to be listened to. He had a purpose to live, a reason to be heard. His voice and music touched millions of lives and may have saved hundreds of broken love affairs. He was that good.

And the voice that really became Frank Sinatra was all due to a larynx breakdown and Ava Gardner.

Breakdowns come and go. Ava came along, stirred the pot of Frank's soul, and became the prime ingredient of bel canto.

Frank had been singing and trying to sing bel canto ever since he had been taking lessons from John Quinlan, the ex-opera singer-turned-voice trainer. He had instilled bel canto in Frank right at the beginning of his career. Frank was able to capture the style of bel canto, but there was also a feeling that comes with bel canto that only some of the great opera singers are able to attain. But for a jazz singer to do this with only a few minutes of time is almost unheard of. Billie Holiday had that style. Mable Mercer and even Ella Fitzgerald could also produce that style of singing. Frank Sinatra put that together right after his fall from grace as a movie and singing star in the late forties. What finally pushed him into the bel canto mode was this unrelenting love affair with Ava Gardner.

Their on-again, off-again relationship and the great love that they had for each other was never really consummated.

No, the sex act, that was always an explosion, like two ferocious tigers meeting for the first time and doing battle for supremacy.

What they could never bring about was the love, the caring, and the giving that two people can share with each other. A sustainable love that could withstand the trials and tribulations that go with every married couple. Some couples can roll with the shock waves of this turbulence; some cannot. There takes a certain inner strength for one to give in to the other. Not always, but at certain times one has to take over for the other, and this giving in to each other after time becomes so imperceptible that the bond created can never break.

Many have found that inner strength, but Frank and Ava

never found the art of giving in one to the other. This is like a dance where one leads and the other follows, and then they reverse roles and allow the other to lead and the other to follow. A dance of give-and-take.

This was the love that they both hungered for but never could find with each other. Neither one was willing to truly give in to the other.

This was the relationship that began Frank's true bel canto. Bel canto is not just the phrasing or the perfect "a" pronunciation or the clear "t," the silent "s." Bel canto is all this and more. Bel canto became something that he had lived; something that had stirred his soul; something that he could taste and almost touch but never could put words to the feeling. The words became alive, because he had lived them. That feeling became alive because one could say that he "willed" that feeling. That special something had forged itself into his very being, and he would and could only show that on stage, in song.

The voice and that feeling were almost there in the beginning of his career because of whatever happened to him in his early childhood and the special training from Quinlan. But Ava Gardner pushed what happened to the voice, the sound and the emotion after *From Here to Eternity,* to its zenith.

After *From Here to Eternity*, the great comeback began.

This was also the same time that the Ava relationship began to crumble with the divorce in 1957 ending the marriage, yet the love they had for each other never ended.

This was the love affair that really and truly began Frank's bel canto. A ferocious love affair, like two antagonists circling each other, they could meet and talk and make intense love, and yet, in this splendor of lovemaking, the outcome was unrequited love.

All you have to do is listen to his music before 1953 and after 1953. Listen to the recording of "In the Wee Small Hours of the Morning," and you will hear bel canto. You can feel the pain of lost love, the pain of unrequited love.

This was the time that Frank's relationship with Nelson Riddle began. Frank had been asked to leave Columbia Records, and after *From Here to Eternity* he contracted with Capitol Records.

This was the time that everything changed. For Frank, this began his metamorphosis. The time that the meteoric star that had almost collided, sputtered, and died, began to rise again and never stopped.

Nelson, born in New Jersey, not too far from Hoboken, also had a dominating mother, and his first marriage may have lasted longer than Frank's, but like Frank's, ended in divorce. He also was a lonely man who drank too much and philandered too much.

Nelson, like Frank, was attached to the classics. They both grew up on them, and these classics became the mainstay of their friendship and their strength for music as singer and arranger.

They both spoke the same language as far as music was concerned. This was an arrangement made in heaven.

Frank stirred again, his face still wet with tears. As he pulled himself up using the bookshelf for leverage, he reached down again and picked out a song sheet that he had not seen in years, one of the first songs he had ever sung to her, "When You Awake."

Frank recorded the song in 1947 and had just started this romance with Ava. They had just spent the night in her place, and she began to pester him about singing a song to her. Usually he would have resisted because he never had done that, only a snippet here and there to his kids or Nancy.

But he could not say no to her. He thought a minute or two, and then for some reason he did not pick one of the classics; instead, he picked this one song, this song that never really went anywhere but described the moment that they were in. The lyrics described how she looked to him at this moment, gloriously beautiful, eyes shining, kneeling in front of him with only a negligee over that beautiful body. He had other thoughts on his mind but he began:

"When you awake, the day takes a bow at your door,

When you awake, the sun shines like never before,

Cloud soaked with rain finds it hard to explain to the earth below,

They can't let it rain for then it would stain a heavenly show, you make it so,

When you awake, you open the eyes of my heart,

When you awake, my day really gets its great start,

All the winds and the birds join the simple refrain of a rippling stream,

My world becomes a midsummer night's dream, when you awake."

He always had that ability to pick the right music, and this was the perfect song to sing to her at this time at this special moment.

He remembered her kneeling on the floor of her living room just a few feet away from him. He had propped himself against the couch and almost whispered to her these words that made her a goddess in his eyes. She slowly began to form tears in her eyes and as the song went on, she came closer to him, placed her arms around his waist, and rested her head on his chest.

He could feel the warmth of her body and as he slowly continued to sing, his desire for her came over him, and yet he knew, he knew instinctively, that this was some magical moment. A moment that did not need disturbing. This moment only needed closeness and quiet. This was a special type of lovemaking. This had nothing to do with the sexual activity; this had to do with the moment and the words and two people who were madly in love with each other. As their eyes met a special bonding happened.

This moment may have been the only time in both their lives that this kind of intimacy had occurred or would ever occur again. A moment of perfect love that very few people ever find or really understand.

They both sat there on the floor, not saying anything, holding on to each other, both afraid to make the first move or the first sound. Words were not necessary. A moment of bliss. They had been blessed, and the world had said okay on this moment in time, this moment of unbridled love.

They stayed this way for several moments after he had finished singing. She was the first to move, and as she turned to him with those beautiful wet green eyes, she whispered, "Thank you," brushed her cheek against his, kissed him lightly, and arose and left the room.

Frank knew that something special had happened at that moment. This had never happened to him before. Just sitting, holding on to the most beautiful woman in the world and not having sex was unheard of. He had never done that before.

And yet he knew that he wanted to do this "holding" again and again, just hold her. No words, no sexual lovemaking. Only her body close to him, tenderly, warm, knowing that she needed him, and he needed her.

He wanted to be needed. He wanted to be part of someone's life that would make a difference. A difference not only in his life but also in her life. He could give that to his children, but he had never found that woman who could make him part of her life . . . until now.

As she walked away he knew something had happened to him. This was the moment. Not only the moment, but also this was the woman. She was the one that would make everything all right. He wanted her, he needed her, and he also realized she needed him.

At that moment in time, he thought that this special love was about to happen; this was to be the perfect love affair. He glowed inwardly.

However, this special love never did, never would, and never could.

Too much had happened in his life and hers that destroyed the chance of that perfect love. And neither one would bend to the other and surrender for that love.

All he had was "When You Awake" and the memory of lost love.

The tears began again and the sobbing was like a child who had lost his puppy and the world was going to come to an end. The crying was of despair, knowing that one could never go back, that one could never find that special place again.

The sobbing and anguished breathing would last for several minutes.

His mind began to travel at the speed of sound, bouncing from one part of time to another. Ricocheting from Ava to Nancy to Nelson, to his mother, to his children. Just short moments of time that had represented so much when they occurred, yet were only quick flashes into a life filled with every form of human emotion. Flashbacks that took only seconds to view but had been a lifetime of ups and downs. After Ava, the throat, and *From Here to Eternity*, his career only rocketed upward.

Throughout his life, Frank had always been in charge, always been in command of his destiny. Defying Mom on his singing career until she gave in and purchased for him his own microphone and amplifier. Mom gave him her blessing as only she could with a slight slap on the face after her pronouncement. The queen always spoke this way.

Leaving Harry for Tommy, and then leaving Tommy to go on his own, to jump ship, to leave the safety of the nest and fly on his own. That is what was his burning desire, to be up there, to be Number One!

He was the first one to go, the first one to leave the protection of a preeminent band, the first to stand alone, alone to be a man and his music.

And he became an American success. An icon.

Recordings, the stage, movies—it was all about the American dream, the dream that every kid in America has for making the dream come true. Some do, some don't. You have to have that desire, that drive, that thirst for success that keeps you going until you taste the water of life, and for Frank, he wanted to drink the whole well. He never had enough.

"Ava, Ava," he moaned as he stirred from this reverie and began to focus more on that tempestuous relationship that for him seemed to last a lifetime.

"Ava, Ava," he cried again as he slipped down to the floor moaning as if in great pain. His chest began to heave with great deep breaths. He was fighting for air. He slowly arose holding on to his chest, heaving as if he had run a hundred yards.

He made himself walk across the room to the large window facing the pool and patio. He grabbed on to the large cushioned chair, sank slowly into the cushion, reached over for a cigarette, lit it, and took that first long drag, then he looked out into nothing in particular and began to flashback again.

The first time he met her was after she had married Mickey Rooney. He had seen pictures of her in some movie magazines, but his actual first meeting was on the movie lot.

She was walking across the street, and he called after her. He could not get over how beautiful she was. He had always had a way with the ladies, and the word *shy* was not in his vocabulary. He forgot what they had spoken about, but she refused to go out with him, being a married man and all. In fact, she was rather cold to him. She did not give him the brush, but there really was a chill in the air after her departure.

After that brief meeting, Frank was more convinced than ever he wanted to take her out and bed her down.

He would meet her again from time to time at various parties. She became easier to talk with, but she never said yes to his advances.

She divorced Mickey, then married Artie Shaw whom Frank despised. After that divorce, Frank began a crusade to capture her. The crusade ended the night they both entered the desert and blew up the town.

From that time on they began to be seen everywhere.

Frank stirred again in his chair, arose, went over to a cabinet against the wall, turned over a tumbler, filled the glass with ice, and poured himself a Jack Daniels and slowly sipped the fiery liquid.

Chapter Ten

Ava's Turn

He retreated back to the chair, stood there, and remembered his home in Palm Springs. That was where he began to immortalize her. He literally plastered the walls with pictures of her. There was nowhere in that house that you did not see a picture of her; even the bathroom had her pictures. She became his obsession, his goddess. He had even purchased the statue they made of her in *The Barefoot Contessa* and had her placed in a prominent spot in the patio area.

The time he began his pursuit of Ava was just about the same time that he began to crumble from his Hollywood perch, and everything else seemed to follow. This was also about the same time that she began her ascent onto the Hollywood movie scene and was on the way to becoming an international star.

As he sank in the chair, he tried to think if there was any period of time that they were completely happy. These were the times he wondered why they had even been brought together. Sexually, they were attracted to each other, but mentally, where real love has to grow, they could not even get off the ground. They could go 2 or 3 days, and then a rift would begin. He would start, or she would start. One would begin with a word or a look, then a crash of words, calling each other every name under the sun. Then as suddenly as the lovemaking started, they would clash and leave each other. Most of the time Frank was the one who would plead to come back and start over again.

Pity me, I need you, he thought. Sad, but he did need her. Even at this time, some 40-odd years later, he could still feel the need for her.

He tried to push her out of his mind as he had tried to do for so many years, but there were times he just could not do that. Those were the times he became like an animal, drinking too much, crying, screaming, and many times wrecking rooms, then spiraling down into a bottomless pit of anguish and despair.

His friends who were always there for him would look in on him from time to time to make sure he did not hurt himself. They would talk about his despair, but no one could help him. No one could talk to him or even bring the subject up. They all knew that Ava was the one who had precipitated the outbreak. They also knew she put the music in his soul.

His screams of "Ava, Ava, Ava" would come through the walls as they sat around waiting for the tirade to end so that they could put him to bed, and then begin to put the room in order.

He stirred and began to remember some of the songs that she enjoyed hearing him sing. She loved his singing, but there were a few tunes that she loved better than others.

He stood up, picked up his glass, finished the drink, took a quick drag on a cigarette before putting it out, and slowly began to walk back to the piano. As he stood there and looked at all the song sheets strewn over the floor, he eased himself down in a squatting position and began to rummage through them looking for certain song sheets.

There in front of him was the song sheet "The Very Thought of You." He stared at the music sheet, and then in a whisper, he slowly moved his lips. "The very thought of you and I forget to do the very ordinary things that I ought to do. I see your face in every flower, your eyes in stars above . . ." He stopped and brought his head down. He began to shake his head from side to side as if to try to be rid of this agonizing pain that kept throbbing in his head. He pleaded for the pain to go away, for her to go away, but he was so deeply entrenched with her that nothing at this time would make her leave.

He gave in to his thoughts as they traveled from one place to another where he had seen her, visited with her, or even heard that she was living over these last 40-some-odd years.

Then everything cleared, and he remembered an evening in Las Vegas. He was still married to Nancy, and Ava and Frank were trying to stay away from the newspaper guys who followed them and pestered them wherever they went. This was still the time when marriage was sacred and no one dared to get a divorce without being ostracized.

Frank and Ava were doing the affair right up front, right before the whole world. They really could not help themselves. They thought they were really in love with each other. Frank knew he was no longer in love with Nancy. He was not sure why but he had left Nancy awhile ago, he only knew that he wanted to be with Ava. They were in love. Screw the rest of the world. They were going to be together and nothing and nobody was going to stop them.

One of his cronies had rented a two-story duplex somewhere in the outskirts of Las Vegas. This was to be a private affair. She had come in earlier in the day and went to the Sands but was able to hide from the reporters and escape them, making her way to their quiet rendezvous.

Frank had to stay in Los Angeles and finish up some business transactions. After dinner he left by himself, made sure no one was following him, and began his ride to Las Vegas to meet Ava.

After several hours of driving he could see the lights of Vegas in front of him. As he approached the city limits he pulled over to a gas station, pulled out the directions to this duplex, and began to make his way to his lover.

She had been difficult at the beginning but his constant attention to her broke her down, and that trip in the desert cemented the relationship. They could not get enough of each other now. They were lovers and would have been content to be left alone for the rest of their lives. If they had been born and raised like the rest of us, perhaps things could have been different, but for Frank and Ava, this love affair was not to be. The whole world was watching and waiting. They were always under inspection.

As he arrived at the house, he could only see a few lights on the driveway and in the house. He wondered why because she usually loved having the house lit up like a Christmas tree. The house gave the appearance of no one being home. If he had not seen her car in the driveway, he would have assumed that she was not there.

As he inserted the key into the front door and swung it open, he could hear himself singing, "The very thought of you . . ." The house was new to him so he had to get his bearings. He cried out, "Ava, Ava, I have arrived," in a joking manner.

Still no answer, only his voice being sung in the background.

As he slowly got used to the dimness of the house, he spotted her shoe on the floor, then a few feet in front of that, the other shoe. He smiled as he suspected she was leaving him a trail.

As he placed the two dozen roses he had brought in on the floor next to one of her silk stockings, he loosened his tie, took off his hat and jacket, and dropped them on the floor.

She had seemed to undress as she made her way to the bedroom on the upper floor. Beside each article of clothing she had placed a candle on the floor or on a step so he could find his way to her.

Frank looked at his lover's message on the stairs and smiled and began to hum to the song in the background. He wanted to do the same thing, take his clothes off piece by piece, but he decided not to. He continued to walk slowly and just let this romantic gesture become part of this rendezvous.

There at the top of the stairs was her dress, and then, undergarments, bra and panties.

He could feel his body tingle with excitement as he slowly continued his journey. He had been with many women and had sex in the strangest places, but this had never happened to him. He was being led on a path of clothing, perfume, and sexual intrigue. When he was in the middle of the climb up the stairs he had noticed that her perfume seemed to be part of the air he was breathing. She had sprinkled some here and some there to make for a more romantic evening.

He was being led into a den of sexual intrigue, a night of romantic interlude. A night he would never forget if he lived hundreds of years.

This was one night that would stay with him forever. Many

times when he sang his songs at studios, concerts, wherever, this one night would enter his mind and the words that he sang would capture the night again and again. He had never before been enticed in this manner. In fact, this was probably the first time in his life that any woman had been the aggressor in such a delicious way—in any way.

He was simply captivated by the whole scene that was being played out before him.

As he reached the bedroom door, he could hear silence, and then another one of his songs on record being placed on the record player to continue the musical interlude. He also heard a distinct pop.

He opened the door gently, and there she was sitting on the bed with her legs crossed, in a lovely but flimsy negligee. She was smiling as only she could, and her eyes were like bright shining stars that lit up her face with a special glow. She had two glasses of sparkling champagne in her hands, one that was extended out to him.

The room was dimmed ever so slightly and after puffing on his cigarette a few times the room took on the look of a perfect rendezvous.

He slowly walked over to her, shook his head slowly in disbelief, and the excitement of seeing her this way coursed through his body. He had only one thought on his mind—of ripping that flimsy gown off of her, undressing her, and making passionate love, but stopped because this was not the right thing to do that. She had choreographed this whole scene, and now she had to continue to direct and to lead him in whatever way she had planned in her pretty mind.

"Hello, Frank, I'm glad you could make it," she quietly

whispered. She gently arose, gave him one of the glasses of champagne, kissed him gently on the lips, raised her glass, and proposed a toast to this special night of bliss.

"To us. May this night be the first of many," she whispered lovingly in his ear. After that, she took another sip of champagne, and then placed her glass down gently on the night table beside the bed.

She slowly glided over to him and began to undress him. As she took off his shirt, he could feel the light sheen of sweat over his lean torso as he moved. She seemed to take forever, one button at a time, very slow movements, sometimes kissing his eyes, his mouth, his cheek, or slowly brushing herself against him, each action adding to the game she was playing. This was an evening of romance, music, champagne, lovemaking, an all-encompassing passionate night of bliss.

As she gently spoke to him and began to remove his clothing from his body, button-by-button, piece-by-piece, Frank was in ecstasy. Attempting to hold back, waiting for the right moment, waiting for the moment that she would tell him that now was the time that he could now enter into this sexual playground and begin to participate. To become an equal partner in this explosion that was going to take place and that would never leave them the same as before they had met in this room.

His thoughts flew back to the way her arms had wrapped around him into heat, into passion. He touched, wantonly, even greedily, her long, limber body, taking and accepting all that she gave him. His breath shuddered as he watched her every move. Every touch of hers brought him to a new crescendo. They both began to touch, to kiss, to nibble. This was clearly her party as she began to tease him with every part of her body and her hands, those gorgeous hands that could do no wrong as she touched and caressed every part of his body, bringing him from one level of excitement to another. He was trying with all his power not to thrust himself on her because he had never, never been made love to this way before, and he greedily wanted more.

Finally, after several minutes of this intense lovemaking, he could hold back no longer. He slowly pulled her toward him, and in one motion, he exploded inside her leaving them both gasping and wanting more. They continued in this torrid fashion, not wanting this moment to end.

Could this be wrong to have such thoughts, such wonderful, exciting visions? How could this be, when they loved so completely? He wanted her heart, but oh, he wanted her body, as well, and he could find no shame in all that they were doing.

Frank said, "Watching, remembering, wondering if she wanted me as much as I wanted her. We never did find out! Why wasn't it to be?"

Then Frank went blank. This was so unconventional to his style of having sex and making love that for the first time in his life he could not say a word. He just let everything happen.

After that day was over and for many years that followed, even as this afternoon of mourning was going on, he could look back and remember each detail of that night as if it had happened yesterday. That was a night to remember forever. That was a sexual gift given only to very few in the universe, and Frank and Ava had been recipients of that extraordinary evening.

The caresses, the kisses, the gentle moaning, the touching, the gentle biting, each sexual gesture was registered in his mind. He had played this scene in his mind over and over again, especially on stage, singing to an audience and yet still wrapped up with Ava and remembering that heavenly night. In some ways that night was his curse, yet in his mind, he thought that night was also a gift that few mortals ever attain.

He did not know how long the lovemaking had lasted, but he did know that he had met his match in this act of love. She was as ferocious and as gentle as he was. They each took a turn to lead the other to the next exotic high. One crescendo after the other, first Ava, and then Frank. The lovemaking seemed relentless and unending.

Yet when the lovemaking did end, they were both spent, exhausted, done in, and somehow, they knew that something else was going on. They knew that something special had happened that night. They both knew that this night might never happen again, and so they wanted to continue, but could not.

This night of lovemaking was over, so they reached for each other, gently whispering words of love to each other, sat up with their backs to the headboard, and when Frank had reached over for a sheet to cover them both, they embraced and tried to make themselves into one body, holding on to each other in fear that this moment would end. They both hoped that this evening could go on and on and on.

They remained snuggling for a good long time. They both had dozed off and when they awoke, they smiled at each other, expressed love and fidelity to each other, slowly extended their bodies on the bed, never letting go of each other, pulled the sheet over themselves, and fell asleep on the romance of the evening.

Frank stirred from his squatting position and remembered the last words of the song "The very thought of you . . . my love."

He bowed his head and as his chin gently rested on his chest, he whispered her name over and over again. "Ava, Ava, Ava . . ."

For several moments he remained still, completely entrenched with her and the night in Vegas. He thought lovemaking in its perfection. She had lured him, enticed him, and then engulfed him in a flame of love that he had never attained and never would come close to attaining again. Fortunately for both of them, he also had been up to the challenge and after initially entering into that sexual interlude and being aroused as never before, he was able to gently and lovingly perform sexual prowess as he had never done before.

Frank could almost say to himself that this was the first, and perhaps the last, time that his sensual awareness was in such a state of lucidity that to this day he could go back and remember almost every movement of that romantic encounter. Even right now, as he thought about that evening, he became aroused, and his body tingled with the excitement of those moments.

Frank had reached paradise, and he knew in his heart of hearts that Ava was right there with him, smiling, and nodding her head in affirmation.

He slowly came out of his reverie and went to reach for another cigarette and remembered his promise to himself not to smoke until after the show. He slowly eased himself back again to that squatting position and began to rummage through the music sheets once more.

Not too far away from his arm's reach he picked up a packet of music sheets that were paper clipped together.

He smiled as remembered the time he had put them all together. They were some of her favorite songs of his singing.

"I'm Gonna Sit Right Down and Write Myself a Letter," "All of Me," "Wrap Your Troubles in Dreams," and "Just One of Those Things."

They really were not love ballads; they were the kind of songs that had a certain bounce to them, a certain joy to them. They were playful tunes that expressed love but not in such a serious tone such as "When You Awake" and "The Very Thought of You."

She could play those songs over and over. To her they were intoxicating, and many times when he saw her listening to these tunes, she would have this far-off look that took her away from the reality of life and brought her to another level where no one could enter and she could be isolated from everyone. During these times and for only a few moments, she was in another world where no one could touch her.

Not even Frank!

Chapter Eleven

Wee Small Hours

As Frank placed this "package" of song sheets over to his left, he happened to spot some other work sheets among the many song sheets dispersed over the floor.

Many times in working a show or a recording, the arranger would give him these work sheets to bring home so Frank could review them and review them and review them. Even the old tunes had to be gone over in his mind and soul so that the best interpretation of that song would come out of his lips for his audience to feel and hear.

Frank became the arranger of his music. He was a perfectionist, and all the tunes that were picked for a recording had to meet with his approval. No one could say to him "Let's do this one, or let's do that tune." No! The only way to approach Frank with some ideas for a recording of an album was to present him with "work sheets" of the tunes that the arranger had put together that he felt would be suited for Frank's voice and that perhaps his fans would be interested in hearing.

At the beginning of his career, and up to the present, any album or show that Frank did had to tell a story and have a style of its own. One did not just throw songs together because Frank had learned well from Tommy and always took care of his audience.

The music that went into any one of these productions had to have some cohesion, not just a helter-skelter of tunes sung only for the sake of singing. Frank was always aware of his audience. They always came first, and he wanted to make sure that he gave them his best. The music had become his. And the audience received his music with love and enthusiasm.

He reached over, stretched a little more, and pulled up the work sheets of "In the Wee Small Hours." The sheets had yellowed a bit, and the rips and scuffmarks on some of the first few sheets and the sketch for the cover of the album had footprints on them. They were not in good shape.

He again began to shake his head back and forth mournfully as he looked at the sketch of the proposed front cover of the album.

A rather dim street with hazy lights coming from lampposts along the street, buildings on the other side of the street, and Frank Sinatra, cigarette in hand, shirt untied at the collar with the tie pulled down a bit, his hat tipped back on his head ever so slightly, and a look of despair on his face.

A perfect setting for the perfect singer in this musical embrace of lost love.

Frank also remembered when Nelson had suggested this album and what had occurred that evening.

The first thing Frank remembered were those nights when the voice had gone and the career was almost over and only Ava was waiting for him, but she was in Africa. He could not count the nights that he walked and walked and smoked cigarette after cigarette on the streets of New York City.

And alone, always alone.

He was desperately pleading for a comeback. Screaming over and over in his head for another break, another chance, and another way to get back to the top. He wanted to show them all that his career was not over. Only a blip in time for Frank Sinatra, only a sore throat.

And he did show them all after *From Here to Eternity*.

But it cost him. It cost him dearly.

He lost Ava!

He found out that Nelson had already spoken to Frank's manager, proposing this album. There had been discussion on the album and some of those meetings became rather heated. Nelson was very sure that this album was made for Frank. And now was the time to record this music. The time was a few years after the Oscar and Frank's comeback had begun. The voice had come back, perhaps better than ever. And Ava had done to him what no one else was able to do; she had made him a singer of bel canto. In a mysterious way, that relationship, with all its ups and downs, wove itself into Frank's psyche and became part of Sinatra.

Now Frank had his own style of singing, and this showed when he first began to sing during the Dorsey days. The voice only improved when he left to be on his own, and spiraled out of control just about the time Ava came into his life. And then something happened after the vocal chord fiasco. Just like a bone becomes stronger after a break, so did his voice. He could not reach the high notes of earlier days, but it carried more resonance, more timbre. As Nelson said, Frank's voice became a viola. And with the Ava love affair in shreds, his voice took on the quality and truer meaning of bel canto. As Bono said in his introduction for Frank at the Grammies, ". . . His songs are his home and he lets you in . . . To sing like that, you gotta have lost a couple a fights . . . To know tenderness and romance, you have had to have your heart broken."

FRANK GARIBOLDI

Nelson had observed Frank's career and with his masterful gift as arranger and friend, could sense the songs that were made for Frank; the combination was truly a marriage made in heaven. They had been together for 2 or 3 years now. Thrown together by Capital Records management.

Nelson had learned in the past 3 years never to thrust anything on Frank. Nelson had to suggest, and Frank had to review and approve. Frank never let anyone dictate his life, especially the music. Frank's mother had tried to do so many years ago, and he had walked out on her. Frank had an uncanny ability to pick the right song for the moment, and Nelson had learned this ability of Frank's right from the beginning. Frank was never the easiest person to conduct or to arrange for. He never just did what he was told to do. Frank knew himself better than anyone else and wanted the music to be just so. There were very few times that Frank let Nelson have his way. And this was to be much later in their relationship.

Frank always admired what Nelson suggested. The album *The Wee Small Hours* was no different. Yet this was a heavy one.

Ava had left him a few years ago, and although he was still trying to make their love stick, every time they tried, it ended in disaster. And every time Frank came back from one of these episodes, he would go into a dark mood, drinking too much, breaking things, yelling and screaming at friends. These episodes were always an ugly time in his life, yet somehow, his singing was the best.

During this time he was able to grasp the essence of the words and music. He became the lost lover, the poor waiting soul, and the jilted person. He became the recipient of unrequited love.

Unrequited love put him back on the charts again and began a meteoric rise that made those few years of inconsistencies a blip, a blip in the life of Frank Sinatra.

As he sat there the sun was beginning to disappear in the background. Yet he remained seated on the floor with Nelson's work sheets in front of him.

They brought him right back to the day that Nelson approached him and suggested that these songs were made for him and that he should consider doing this LP. Nelson said later that he had this LP in mind for a long time before bringing it to Frank. Nelson knew that the songs represented Frank's pain of the last few years, yet he also knew that the combination of these songs was written especially for this time, specifically for Frank. Frank had not paid much attention at that time.

Frank remembered that when he received these work sheets, they had just finished a recording session and he was on his way out the door. He had listened to Nelson, and then casually stuck them under his arm and planned to look at them later that evening.

The following morning around 4 a.m. when he arrived home, he happened to spot the work sheets on his bed, just where he had left them after the afternoon's recording session. As he loosened his tie and began to unbutton his shirt, he picked up the work sheets and slowly began to read the program outlined by Nelson:

In The Wee Small Hours—Mood Indigo—Glad to Be Unhappy—I Get Along without You Very Well—Deep in a Dream—I See Your Face before Me

He stopped in his tracks as he finished reading the other titles. Some were very well known and others had come and gone but were still songs of loneliness, lost love, or eternal hope.

And through them all ran the thread of Ava. She was in every title, almost every word. This was all that Frank could feel.

He threw the work sheets down and began to stomp on them with his feet, almost tearing them apart and cursing and screaming at Nelson for even suggesting that he record these songs. He had a mind to call Nelson up but something stopped him.

Suddenly a weird feeling came over him.

As he looked at the work sheets on the floor, he actually became calm in a matter of seconds. Something strange was happening. The anger left him, and he stooped down, slowly picked up the sheets, sat on his bed, and began to review the suggested songs by Nelson.

As he sat on the floor he remembered that night as if it were yesterday. There had been other times in his life when things like that had occurred to him and he knew instantly never to let go of the moment without looking at that particular situation from all sides.

He was being told something, and he had to listen, and he had to review the song sheets. Something special was going on.

His mind quickly returned to the bedroom as he sat and reviewed the works sheets of *In the Wee Small Hours*.

He quickly realized that Nelson had placed the songs in an order that almost told a story. They weren't just haphazardly thrown together to make an album. With a few exceptions he liked what he saw. They were all highly emotional songs, and each one deserved a special review, a special reverence.

And through each and every song and almost every word

as he remembered the words, Ava kept pounding in his head. If he decided to do this album, he would be baring his soul. He might be vulnerable to the world, and he had never done that before. There had been hints of vulnerability in the past but never like this, all at once, one song after the other, almost no time to take a breath, only short gasps of air. He had to think about this one.

He slowly slipped from the top of the bed to the floor with his back against the bed. He had been tired when he arrived home, but now he was wide awake. All his musical senses seemed to be vibrating at once, and he knew this moment had to be looked at from all sides because this was great music, and he would never have a chance like this again.

He looked at the first song and remembered the first few lines and whispered, "In the wee small hours of the morning, when the whole wide world is fast asleep, I lie awake and think about the girl and never think of counting sheep . . ."

"Shit, I remember walkin' the streets of New York City only a few years back when nothin', nothin', was goin' right. The whole world was fallin' apart. No movies! No recordings! No Ava! She was in some stupid fuckin' place in Africa, and I was alone, alone, alone," he screamed out, and the words echoed back to him making him shiver from head to toe.

"What the hell do you do when everything you have is goin' down the fuckin' tubes? When all you have is yourself to hang onto and nobody out there really gives a shit?

"All ya have is yourself and all ya can do in the wee small hours is walk and walk and talk to yourself. Ya find yourself goin' forward and backward and backward and forward; nothin' makes sense. And shit do ya think? All ya think about is what could have been, what should have been, and nothin' ya think about makes any sense. It's like a cesspool in your head, a lotta shit; nothin' makes any sense. And then when you're really desperate, ya pray a little. Maybe God can help.

"Now in the wee small hours of the morning, she comes to mind more often than not. When am I gonna get rid of her? How the hell does he want me to sing these songs?" he screamed, as he threw the sheets across the bedroom and they scattered here and there.

Before he moved from the side of the bed to pick them all up, that feeling came to him again. *Don't let this moment go by. There's something going on; don't let this moment go by without a good thorough review.*

As he gathered the work sheets, the title of this recording came into view *In the Wee Small Hours of the Morning.* "Now that I understand," he murmured as his mind again traveled to the canyons of New York City when he had walked his fool head off in the wee small hours.

"'Glad to Be Unhappy,' now does that make sense? Well, it does now. Just glad to be around, just glad for the turnaround in the career and unhappy because she is not with me. She's probably out with that Spanish bullshit fighter. Why the fuck does she wanna be with him and not me?"

From nothing to everything, to almost nothing in a short 10 years. "What the hell happened?" he screamed, and his voice vibrated in the bedroom from one wall to another as the sound echoed all the way out of the room, through the door, and found itself in the vastness of the house and died.

Was the love affair really all over? He did not want it to be, but at this time, it sure looked like the final act for him.

His mother and father kept telling him, "I told you so." A few of his so-called friends, the hangers-on, had left him.

Actually, Nancy was the only one who gave him any consolation. But she wanted him to forget the whole thing, like a bad dream. It worked for a while. "Come home, I still love you, the kids need you, come home."

Nancy was always there. But that's not what he needed. She was always smothering him. She wanted him to come home to be with the kids. She was always telling him he could find other things to do, get another job in the show business world. She saved some money. They could go back to Hoboken. Hoboken! Are you kidding? Hell, that's not what he wanted.

He needed the excitement of the crowd, the "rush" that comes from taking an extra bow because the song had come out better than expected; he needed the screaming and the yelling, "Frankie, Frankie, Frankie!" He needed the fans; he wanted to be number one.

This was his dream, and no one, not even Nancy, was going to stop him from getting back on top. No one!

The kids he missed. He knew that somehow he had screwed up with them.

He was glad to be unhappy. He could not remember a time in his life when he had been really happy. Happiness had come in spurts. As he looked back, unhappiness seemed to be his lifestyle.

This left him rather subdued. He had been sitting on his haunches, and now he slowly stretched his legs out, crossed one over the other, and calmly came back to review the rest of the work sheets.

He had scattered the sheets haphazardly on the floor in

front of him so he reached down and picked the first one that touched his fingers. "'Mood Indigo.' Now that's the Duke's prime song. Why the hell does Nelson want me to sing it?

"You ain't been blue, No! No! No! You ain't been blue, till you've had your Mood Indigo." He gently said the words as his mind traveled back to Hoboken, his birth city. He was an only child, in a world where children abounded, with almost every family having three or four children. Picked on wasn't what happened to him. Shit on was more like the world he lived in.

A few friends, but he always seemed to be by himself with his dream. The dream sustained him. The dream gave him the will to go on. His was a lonely childhood. Only his dreams kept him going. When he would see Bing Crosby on the screen or hear him on the radio, that is when the big dream came and he would not let anyone or anything bust that bubble. The dream was first, and everything else was second. Wife, family, friends—no one would get in the way of his dream. No one!

His dreams were his way out!

"I see your face before me. Shit I can't go anywhere without seeing her. She's in all the papers, magazines, in my head, all over."

He slowly arose from that position. His behind was getting sore and he wanted to rest on something a little softer than the floor. He slowly picked up all the song sheets, moved to the bed, and placed himself in a sitting position back against the headboard, lit a cigarette, and began his review again.

"'When Your Lover Has Gone.' Man! Nelson really went out of his way to put this one together.

"It Never Entered My Mind," "Ill Wind," "This Love of Mine."

As Frank looked at the work sheet back in his room he remembered the recording of "This Love of Mine" as if it were yesterday. Something happened on that recording that had never happened before. And now the whole thing came tumbling back in the memory banks of his mind.

Nelson, Frank, and all the musicians had gone over this number for some time. They had played the song over and over, so they could put music and words together with as much perfection as is humanly possible. They were now ready.

As Nelson checked the band for their readiness, he glanced at Frank for final approval. Receiving it, he tapped the music stand and the recording began.

As Frank opened his mouth to sing, "This love of mine . . ." there she was, Ava, sitting in front of him. She did not have on anything fancy, just a simple brown skirt with a white blouse and a paisley scarf loosely wrapped around her lovely neck. She was smiling with only her upper teeth showing and her lips were brushed with only a slight tint of lipstick. Her green eyes glistened with rapture and love for Frank. She was looking directly at Frank, never taking her eyes off of him, and pleading for the words of his song to wash over her. Her body did move ever so slightly as the words continued, ". . . goes on and on, though life is empty since you have gone, you're always on my mind though out of sight, it's lonesome through the day but ooh the night . . ."

He felt this warmth begin from the middle of his stomach and spread up and down his body. And as the song continued he began to tremble.

Again, Ava moved gently, leaning forward, listening to the words with great intensity, letting the music intensify the love they had for each other. She closed her mouth, still smiling, still looking radiant while the intensity of her eyes bored right through his heart.

Frank seemed to be in another world, and he knew that this love affair with Ava was never going to end. Maybe when they died, and then who knows, maybe they would meet somewhere in the unknown and keep the affair going. Weird was how he felt. He wanted to stop, but she would not allow him to do so. He seemed to be in a trance. He remembered seeing Nelson and all the guys, but his body was numb.

He did not hear the music. He did not need the music. He was in another dimension.

"I cry my heart out, it's bound to break; since nothing matters let it break. I ask the sun and the moon, the stars that shine, what's to become of it, this love of mine."

As he completed the last words of the song, Ava arose, waved at him, threw a kiss, and ever so gently faded from sight.

Frank had tried many times to bring her back that way, but she never returned. He always knew she was there. He could feel her and almost smell her. He always sang these love songs to her.

The moment was uncanny and surreal. Her appearance in his songs was not new to him, but in this song she lingered throughout the whole melody. The song became bel canto at its finest.

Her lengthy appearance had happened once and that was that, yet it was special!

He put the song sheet down and remembered the angry words that they always threw at each other. They both tried to outshout the other, both of them using the best curse words they had in their vocabulary. And break things? The room was always a disaster after their encounters. She had a habit of throwing things. Either he ducked quickly or she was a bad thrower. "We were lucky we didn't kill each other," he softly whispered.

He looked at his watch and whispered angrily, "Shit, it's almost time to get ready." But he could not get off this reverie that he was in.

He slowly went back to that night in the bedroom, in the beginning of *Wee Small Hours*.

"Ill Wind Blow Away," another torch song he screamed. He rolled off the bed and reached for the phone and began to dial Nelson's number but stopped after the first few numbers. He could not continue dialing.

He stood up straight and glanced at the some of the other numbers, "Dancing on the Ceiling" and "I'll Never Be the Same." "All torch songs, what the hell was Nelson thinking? What does he want me to become? Another Lady Bird? Fuck that shit," as he reached for the phone again.

As he did that, Billie Holiday came into vision, smiling that sad smile, just like she did the last time he saw her in the hospital a few weeks before she died. And as she smiled at him, she was nodding her head up and down slowly and said, "Frank, sing the songs."

He had tried to shake her out of his head, but she wouldn't leave him. Billie stood up from her hospital bed dressed in a white satin gown. As she slowly turned around to face him, she began to sing "Ill wind blow away, let me rest today, you're blowin' me no good, no good!" The song was haunting a song of lost love and a song of a lost life. Billie had been the best interpreter of these types of songs, and Frank had idolized her. When he first started recording he tried to use that style of singing and interpretation of those torch songs given to him by arrangers, and he was able to interpret them in that style.

Never like Billie, though; she lived it.

Frank would too, in a different way.

Frank had lived a rather stormy childhood, but he couldn't compare his life to her life. The drugs, the beatings, they just shit all over her, and yet she was a class act. This was her life; this is what she lived for—the music and the adulation from her fans. Her love of music and her fans were the only things that made her go on.

Frank loved Lady Bird, and he lived for the same things, the same accolades that she did.

As she slowly faded from sight he also knew that this was his life and the only thing that he had ever lived for. The only thing in his life that really meant anything to him, anything at all, was the singing and the audience.

As he found his way to the bar to pour himself a drink, he happened to glance around the room and there she was. Ava's pictures were everywhere, in all sorts of standing and sitting poses. He slowly walked around each room—living room, den, office, kitchen, the hallway, even the bathroom, then back into the bedroom. She was everywhere. He had made a memorial of her right here in his own home. He realized that there were days that he had forgotten that she was all over his walls. Small pictures, big, medium—everywhere.

He slowly wound his way back to the bedroom, drink in hand, and plopped himself on the bed as he muttered, "I've got to do this album. That son of a bitch Nelson, he's right. I've got to sing these fuckin' songs. It's all about my life. My mother, the old man, Nancy, me as a kid, the ups and downs of this fuckin' career of mine, and her, her," he screamed, "damn it, she's all over these songs.

"I've got to do it," he softly said as he began to cry uncontrollably. "Ava! Ava!" he yelled at one of her pictures across the room. He leaped from the bed, threw the work sheets away from him, took two long strides to the wall, and began to pound her picture with the palm of his hand. He only stopped when his hand became red and numb. He then banged his head against the picture a few times. He stopped, tears streaming down his face, his chest heaving from all that furor. As he slowly reached up, he grabbed the top of the picture and tore it off the wall. He turned around, leaned his back against the wall, and slid down to the floor, holding her picture against his chest, and now he really began to sob. They were loud, tearing sobs from deep inside his body. He could hardly catch his breath. This went on for several minutes.

As he gradually came to and the sobs were like whimpers every few seconds, he lifted his head from his knees, looked at the picture, and kissed her on the lips, gently, lovingly.

He was still in love with her.

The torch he carried for her probably would never end, and this was to be his cross for the rest of his life. He would have to carry that torch, just like Billie did.

He now knew without a doubt that he had to record these songs. They were to be a living memory of his past. He truly wanted to put the past to rest. There were too many things going on right now. His whole world had turned around. He wanted to make that dream he had as a kid become a reality, not for 5 or 10 years but for the rest of his life.

"Yes," he yelled at the top of his lungs, "it's time to let the past go. Sing it all out. Get it all out. Screw her and everybody else. I've gotta look out for me. Nothin's changed! I've gotta look out for Frank Sinatra."

He was kneeling at this time, and as he let those words reverberate around the room, he rose and thanked God for the return of his voice.

He was now at peace with himself as he slowly rose from the kneeling position, turned, and placed the picture back on the wall. Then he turned off the lights and in complete exhaustion fell on the bed and was asleep immediately.

Chapter Twelve
The Very Last Time

His legs were getting numb from that squatting position. Gingerly he rose and began to shake his legs, one at a time, and then carefully walked to get the blood circulating again. He smiled as the pins and needles began to ease themselves from his legs. He looked at his watch again—only one-and-a-half hours to go. He began to stretch, arms reaching to the ceiling. His toes extended as far as they could go. He needed a good stretch. He stopped.

As he turned and looked at every wall in the room, he realized there was not one picture of her. He also remembered that the statue of The Barefoot Contessa was now gone from his garden. He had tried to free himself of her but had never been truly successful. He had succeeded in ridding himself of all her gifts, pictures, and anything that even hinted at her presence, and he had become very good at stuffing feelings and desires.

"Ya can get rid of stuff, but ya can't get rid of da memory," he said solemnly.

Perhaps now that she was dead he could really let her go he thought. But there was no great conviction as he pondered those words.

As he stood there he also realized that she had set a certain tone to his career. The true passion in his voice was from her. The bel canto that John had always spoken about and tried to drill into his music only came from her. Could he let her go? Only time would tell.

The years of smoking, drinking, and late hours had hurt the voice. But when he sang a ballad, he could still make the words live. No, not like 20 years ago, but there was still enough there to touch his audience. To bring them back again and again. Ava was still haunting his music.

He straightened himself and began to walk over to the window. As he gazed across his beautiful garden and patio, his mind traveled back to the night he had tried to make one more pitch to keep her, to make her understand that they could work this love affair out.

Every once in a while in that stormy relationship they tried to make a comeback. He was always the first one to try. He was always traveling to where she was. He became angry and jealous over the stories in the papers, over her romances with her leading men or some other "jerk." He was insanely jealous and had almost given his life for her, suicide.

He was going to try once more to bring her back. They had been speaking to each other again. Almost like the old days. This little spark had raised his hopes of getting together again. This was a few years before the final papers of the divorce had been issued and several months before *In the Wee Small Hours* recording.

He paused and remembered that special night in Las Vegas when she had led him into that sexual paradise. Clothes left scattered around the house, the music, the champagne, and then that night of bliss where they committed themselves to each other.

He would never forget that night. He wanted that night back again. He wanted her back again.

He had let all the servants go. This was going to be a perfect night, one of romance, but also one of quiet understanding. He was attempting to perform the same miracle that Ava had performed many years ago at the beginning of their tormented love affair. He was going to be on his best behavior. He really wanted the evening to be perfect. He would have to be strong and hold his sexual advances for the proper time. As far as he was concerned, this was all about putting things back in order between him and her. This was about making the marriage work, making the relationship work.

He had arrived home fairly early in the evening. She was not to arrive until about 9:30 p.m. Her schedule at the studio would keep her there until around 6 or 7 p.m. and by the time she went home to freshen up, she was not to arrive until a few hours later. They always ate late and partied until the wee hours.

He had brought in several dozen white, red, and pink roses and was looking around to make sure that they had been placed in the proper areas of the house so they would actually send the correct message. She was partial to camellias, and so he had a few dozen of those especially flown in, and he was in the process of placing them in the proper areas, a few in the dining area, a few in the main bathroom, some in the bedroom, and the rest in the living room.

The place was now beginning to look just right.

He went into the kitchen to begin to prepare their dinner. She loved his sauce and macaroni and was also partial to prosciutto.

The macaroni, cheese, mushrooms, bread sticks, and prosciutto had just arrived today after being purchased from downtown Bleecker Street in Little Italy. They had good Italian delis in Los Angeles, but nothing like New York's Little Italy. As far as he was concerned they had the best.

He began by wrapping the prosciutto around the bread sticks and placing each one on an oval dish. A dozen would be enough. He then began to make the sauce from scratch—tomatoes, basil, salt, pepper, and some ingredients that only he knew and would never tell anyone else. Frank was famous for his sauce, and Ava could never get enough, dipping bread into the sauce and devouring each piece with gusto.

After the sauce was simmering on the stove, he then proceeded to the dining area to set up the dishes for the meal. As he looked around the dining room, he decided against using this room and went looking for the right space to have this special, special encounter, this special romantic interlude.

He went from one room to another, and then stepped outside on the patio, and as he looked around he found what was to be the perfect spot, the space just outside on the patio. There were a few scattered chairs and tables, but quickly in his mind he saw the perfect setting. Not too far away from the kitchen area. He would ask her to help him with the drinks while he took care of the culinary duties. He was beginning to really get into this.

He quickly rearranged the chairs and tables, placing a clean tablecloth over one of the tables and setting the chairs around so they would look natural. He placed a few camellias in the center of the table, and the roses were placed in other areas of the patio to give the whole area a more relaxed atmosphere.

Frank had this unusual ability not only to arrange his own music and place musical instruments at the right time and place in his songs, but he also had this gift of interior design, knowing where things went in a home so to bring out the best of a certain room. The rooms he lived in and the rooms he played in were always done in exquisite taste. He had this gift, and he always used it well.

After he finished, he looked over the whole scene. Satisfied that the patio was now perfect and to his taste, he gave a quiet sigh and smiled. He then returned to the kitchen to give a quick look at the sauce that was now simmering on the stove. He lowered the flame just a teensy bit, put his finger in the sauce and then directly into his mouth and shook his head with satisfaction. He then placed a cover over the sauce, not covering the pot completely, but leaving just a small space for the heat to remain but not to bubble over. The sauce had to simmer another hour or so.

He gave the scene a second look and nodded with satisfaction.

He then headed for the shower.

Upon leaving the shower he dressed in baby blue slacks, matching loafers, and a white silk shirt. As he placed the shirt over his shoulders he reminded himself to be aware of the sauce; red and white combine well, but not on shirts, especially expensive silk ones.

At about 9:30 p.m. or so he went into the kitchen, checked the sauce one more time, and put water in the pot for the macaroni. He placed the macaroni pot on the stove, put a small flame on underneath, and headed to the bar to chill the champagne and prepare the Barone wine that was to be used for tonight's meal. He wanted to let the wine breathe so that this special liquid would entice both of them on this night of romance.

FRANK GARIBOLDI

Everything was ready! He began to review some things in his head that he wanted to convey to her, but the only thought that came to him was to stay cool. Don't push. Don't go overboard. Be truthful! Make love to her with words. Explain how our love can all work out. Make her understand that the love they have for each other can conquer all sorts of barriers. Use words. Keep your hands off of her. That will come later, he thought.

He repeated again and again, "It's important to remember, to make love to her with words. Use your words in the same way as you do when you sing. Make them have meaning. Love her gently."

As he finished the scene in his mind, he heard the bell ring, and a few moments later, he heard his name being called. "Frank, Frankie, where are you?"

She had arrived.

Chapter Thirteen

It's Over

She was on her way out. What the hell had happened? She was cursing him with every curse word that she could think of. Every saying she could remember her father telling her when she was growing up. She turned in the middle of the driveway screaming at the top of her lungs that this affair was over. No more would she come back; too much pain, too much yelling and screaming. As far as she was concerned, there would be no more men in her life, especially Frank. He was a no-good bastard and deserved only the fires of hell, and now would be a good time to turn on the fire.

She opened the door to her car and cried out into the darkness, "You no-good son of a bitch!" The door slammed shut, the engine started, and with tires screeching, she left him.

Frank was also doing his share of screaming and cursing, and he threw the bottle of Barone wine that was in his hand. "You no-good whore bitch," he bellowed at her.

As he gazed at the patio from his standing position at the window, he could see that ugly scene directly in front of him.

What happened? They had started out with romance and ended in a world war. The evening had ended as all their encounters did. Frank had taken a long time to try to understand what was going on in this relationship, and he never could.

He still did not understand!

He did realize that this was never to be, and yet, he could

and would never stop loving her completely. Removing the pictures from the walls of the house had helped, and yet, the songs that he sang always brought her back.

Even now, staring out the window, he went back to that last night and wondered what went wrong.

When she first arrived, they had embraced, kissed but not too passionately, just enough to get the romantic juices moving. Over the last few years they had seen each other once in a while because he had made the effort to see her and he also had been on the phone more than she, trying to reconcile this crazy love affair. She only called when things were not going right and she needed his help. He always was there for her, hoping beyond all hope to bring her back. He would never stop trying to do that.

When she arrived they kissed lightly and began with small talk. He poured the champagne, offered her prosciutto-wrapped bread sticks, and then invited her out to the patio where they both sat on two cushioned chairs across from each other. The music in the background was of him singing her favorite songs, plus a few others that he knew she liked.

He remembered the scene as if they were sparring. Like boxers in a ring, each one eyeing the other and not really giving an inch.

As he moved again from the window to a chair, he realized that a romance like that would not go anywhere. Each one wanted to be the leader. Each one of them had to have things their way. Each one was unwilling to give an inch. A good relationship requires giving 110 percent of yourself to your partner. If you're not willing to do that, you can only expect disaster.

Both Frank and Ava were so consumed with their own needs that they were unable to give the love to each other that makes relationships work.

He slowly returned to the scene.

He remembered telling her how good she looked and that Spain must be good for her, but that the good old US of A was just as good and a lot closer for them to see each other.

She had nodded, not wanting to enter into that conversation. As far as she was concerned, she would probably never come back to the States, only for visits. She would not give up her citizenship but she certainly was not going to live here. She was more comfortable in Spain and was even considering moving to London. She seemed to be attracted to London and eventually she would wind up moving there permanently.

The conversation had gone from his work to Frank's mother, to the kids, and then to Ava's work. They had finished a bottle of champagne, and the prosciutto bread sticks were gone.

Frank had been the perfect host, pouring drinks, supplying the food as needed, and looking over at the kitchen to make sure all was going well.

They had decided to eat out on the patio, so they both helped to bring out the dishes, silverware, and cheese to the patio table. They both were laughing and beginning to enjoy each other.

As Frank poured the "breathing" Barone wine, Ava came over and touched him on the shoulder and kissed him on the cheek and said in a very soft and tender voice, "Thank you."

Frank was not sure what to do because this move by her took him by surprise, but he quickly regained his composure, finished pouring the wine, and gently reached out with his left hand, touched her face, and said, "Thanks for being here with me."

This was the moment that he hoped and knew would come from this encounter. Now was the right time for the passion that they felt for each other to come out and be aroused. Here was the desperation of two people in need of each other in the most intimate way created, the sexual encounter of a man and a woman.

He quickly pulled her to him, and as they slowly wound their way into the house, they began to take off each other's clothing, leaving a trail all the way into the bedroom, a shoe, a sock, a stocking, dress, pants, everything there on display.

Then in the bedroom with only dim lights glimmering, they continued their lovemaking with complete abandonment. This was the special world that they both lived in, the world that they both cherished. This was the reason that they were attracted to each other. The lovemaking was a need they both wanted and desired. Sexually, they had found the perfect match with each other. They would never find that match again, even though they would try with other partners. The intensity of the perfect lovemaking between two lost souls in need of this desperate love was the perfect aphrodisiac for these two desperate people.

Frank had always been the aggressor in lovemaking, but in this relationship he knew, and she knew, that they were both on equal grounds. So their lovemaking was of equal strength and ferocity. They both craved dominance, and they both were able to allow the lovemaking done to the other without a change in the passion they had for each other. In the bedroom, equality reigned supreme. They both knew this without ever speaking about it. There was no need for words.

This was their meaning of bliss, the perfect consummation of love between a man and a woman. This is what always brought them together. If they could do this forever, then all would be right with the world. If they could only exist in their lovemaking, then life would be perfect for both of them.

Their egos would not let it be, however. Their egos had interfered with their personal relationship.

And that is how this love affair ended, with the ego. His.

After a few hours of torrid lovemaking, they were both exhausted, and as he rose on one elbow to look at this most beautiful of women here on this bed of his, he sarcastically said, "Now how does that stack up with those Spanish bums?"

That did it! She exploded with expletives coming from her mouth in a torrent of rage. There was fire in her eyes as she quickly arose from the bed, turned, and glared at him. There was hatred in those same eyes that only a few minutes ago shone with love and compassion. Now, if looks could kill, Frank would have been dead.

She stood there naked, her body shaking with fury, making her breasts bounce ever so lightly against her chest and making her even more appealing in his eyes. But she had venom in her eyes, and her right hand was balled in a fist, shaking violently toward him while the other was ready to beat him if he even attempted to come close.

She picked up the first thing she could get her hands on and threw it in his general direction. The bottle splattered all over the wall leaving the room filled with the nauseating smell of men's cologne.

Then as she began to retrieve her clothing following the same trail out as she had followed when she had come in, she quickly dressed herself. She knelt or sat and did whatever she could to get dressed as quickly as possible. She desperately wanted to leave, and leave as quickly as she could. She put on her panties first, thrusting her legs into the openings as her mouth never stopped spewing hostilities at him. She tried putting on her bra and gave up. She slammed the bra on the floor and stomped on it with both feet while cursing Frank with all the anger that could come out of her mouth.

She raged over and over again that their affair was finally over, screaming at the top of her lungs, "Over! Over! Over!" With this last shout she gave her bra a final kick that sent the damn thing sailing right across the room landing on the bed, next to the kneeling Frank who was dumbfounded at the scene that was being played out in front of him.

While she was getting dressed, Frank stood up, followed her, and began to do the same.

While this rather awkward dress scene was taking place she never stopped berating him. She shouted at the top of her voice that he was an ungrateful bastard, that he only cared for himself, that he was conceited and afraid. Yes, afraid, because he always had to have his gorilla friends surrounding him. He couldn't make a move without them. She had tried from the beginning to be a good woman and a good wife because she thought she loved him and wanted to please him, but she saw now that he was the most conceited and arrogant bastard that she had ever met.

She had fire in her eyes, and the words spewed out like venom. She wanted to cut him up with words and leave him there completely naked so that the vultures would come and ravage his body.

Her tirade was the reverse passion of a few moments ago. A passion of love turned into a passion of hate, a passion of rage. This was ferocious—love and hate—all in the same pot.

This was truly ugly!

At first Frank was taken aback at the outburst, then he even tried to apologize for saying the wrong thing. His plan to reconcile was going down the sewer.

He was slow on the take, but at last felt he could not let her go on without getting back at her. One part of him told him not to because he realized he had said a dumb and stupid thing. He wanted nothing more than to take the words back. Ava was now half-dressed, halfway through the house, and the words coming out of her were fast and furious. She sounded like a volcano erupting, pure hellfire.

He first tried to apologize for the stupid remark. She was not even paying attention; she was too furious. He tried to grab her arm and hold her so he could try to make some sense of what was happening, but she pulled away and continued to blast him and get dressed at the same time.

As she was getting near the front entrance to his home, he was also dressing as quickly as she was. Somewhere in his head he thought, how the hell is this even happening? And what really took him by surprise is that he also thought this would make a great scene in a movie.

He regained his senses, or maybe he didn't because then he realized the futility of the situation and began to fight back in the only way he knew how. He picked up the bottle of Barone wine, and then took a quick drink to loosen up his vocal chords. His thoughts raced back to the days when he and his mother would go at it tooth and nail, neither one giving an inch. Somehow, his mother always won as she always would. And he had no way of stopping her.

He loved his mother.

He loved Ava.

Realizing that pleading with her was not doing any good, he then took her on face to face, word for word, venom for venom.

There was hatred in both their eyes. They began to spew words from their mouths not one listening to the other, just a blabbering of incoherent language that fell on deaf ears.

The music had stopped and the sauce had been on a little too long. Somehow the smell of burning sauce added to the catastrophe that was occurring.

The overpowering smell of cologne with the burning smell of macaroni sauce only added to the chaotic scene that was unfolding in the Sinatra residence.

She drove away. He collapsed on the floor in tears.

It's over; it's over he kept repeating in his mind. He clasped his hands on his chest trying to open the cavity so more air could go in and allow more room for his heart, because it was getting ready to explode.

Chapter Fourteen
Endings

Frank slowly stirred as he began to come back to reality. His heart was pounding, and his face was wet from tears. He used his hands and his arms to wipe away the tears as he began to refocus himself. He slowly arose, walked over to where he had left the bottle and glass, and poured himself another drink. A good three fingers' worth.

As he picked up and lit the cigarette, he went over to look at the song sheets thrown all over the floor. His heart was pounding rather loudly. He could feel his heart as he began to drink this glass of bourbon. He sipped the liquid down. As he finished his drink, he automatically stubbed out the cigarette and the pounding of his heart gradually began to subside.

He looked at the song sheets on the floor. There must have been 30 or 40, and he had memorized all of them, and perhaps hundreds more. Not bad for a high school dropout he thought. Yet he knew his memory did not come from the high school years. It was this special desire that he had inside, something that told him never give up, never give up!

He had this desire when he was just a young teenager, and now at 75 years of age, he still had the same desire. He could never leave the stage. Never! And she was wrong. He needed those guys around him, not because of fear but because of friendship. He craved that friendship, that camaraderie from the guys, and that special friendship that came from the ladies. Especially now, at his age where the sexual desires were not there as strong as they used to be, he could understand and appreciate the ladies around him just for that special warmth that only a woman can give.

He knew that Hollywood men and women were different. Most of them only wanted notoriety, and Frank somehow always looked for friends with heart, those friends that one could share a laugh, a drink, and a tear when needed.

He may not have done much of that searching for those kinds of friends at the beginning of his career. She was right. He had only the guys around him, but as his career began to really take off, his group of friends began to expand and included the wives of many of the guys, and as time went on, he began to really and truly appreciate these friendships.

They were not "hangers-on" like she screamed at him that night. They were friends and very dear friends at that.

As he looked at the song sheets again, he nodded very slowly and very knowingly that Ava had made a huge impact on the way he sang a song. She had been his teacher without ever giving him a lesson. She had been his mentor without ever talking about music and feelings or desires or high notes and low notes. She had become his source of bel canto.

"If it wasn't for her," he muttered, "who knows what would have happened."

He slowly thought about this for a while, and then began to admit that he would still have been okay after *From Here to Eternity* and the voice was better after that throat fiasco, but, and that was a big BUT, the feeling would not have been there if she had not entered his life.

Was she worth all the pain? Was all this pain and suffering that he had gone through, and was still going through, worth all he accomplished?

He took some time to think about that question. He tried to analyze the question from all different angles and came to the conclusion that there was not really anyone else that had an impact on his voice as much as she had.

He actually had no choice. It was something that happened, and that's all there was to it. It happened.

No lessons! No instructions! Only this feeling between two people. He was not sure what impact he had on her life, but he knew damn well the impact she had on his. She had crawled into his psyche, into his very being, and remained there and only came out in the music, especially those torch songs. Those songs that spoke of high drama, lost love, broken hearts, unrequited love. All he had to do was open his mouth to sing and she was there right in the song. He never had to study, rehearse, do over. All he had to do was sing. His diction never left him, his understanding of the words was always there, and his love of what he was doing would never leave him.

All that came from a special sensibility on how to put all those things together. When he sang, out of nowhere came the emotion, the passion, and the mood change; an outlook, an attitude. This became his gift, to cherish, to love, and sometimes even to hate.

There was an atmosphere that took over his whole being as he sang these songs that could permeate into the very souls of the people listening.

His was not just a voice with words. His was a voice that had been through all the drama, all the chaos, and all the passion that one could go through in a torrid and unconsummated love affair.

One could read about such affairs in the newspapers or books. Many of them ended in terrible tragedy, with the death of one or both lovers.

Somehow with Frank, although he did attempt suicide once or even twice, the tragedy of this affair wound up inside his body, inside his very soul. She became part of him in an unexplainable way.

He could live his life very well. Happy, glad, sad!

Only in the music did she come over and help him. Only in the music was he able to have her and love her. Only in the music was he safe and she was safe with him.

The music was the only place where the world could not get at him. The place where Frank could tell the rest of the world of all the misery and sorrow that had been going on all his life. There in the music and its interpretation did he feel all the suffering of lost love and was able to explain lost love better than anybody else ever could or ever would.

No one else had been through the Ava saga with him. She had entrenched herself into his psyche and now could never be pulled away from him.

This was the torch that he carried, and he carried it well and gave it homage. That was his gift to the world.

Although he never talked about Ava with anyone, Frank knew that he owed her. There were still times that he would curse her and many times when speaking to her on the phone it would end in disaster; yet he knew he owed her.

As this thought coursed through him he also realized that his mother, as much as she opposed his singing, did buy him his first microphone, which pushed him in the right direction. And how about Quinlan? John pulled and pushed and did everything in his power as a voice coach to get the message of bel canto out and to make the song and music belong to Frank and Frank alone.

He owed all three, but the one who got into his voice and got into his psyche was Ava.

There were those times on the stage when he sang "One for My Baby," "Didn't We," "The Very Thought of You," or "Guess I'll Hang My Tears Out to Dry," and many other songs that spoke of desperation, perfect love, and unrequited love. Those were the times she came out of nowhere and was on the stage with him, sometimes just sitting there right in front of him, smiling that special smile of hers, nodding her head in approval, and those green eyes, those special eyes, penetrating right through him.

Yes! He owed her!

That was always Frank at his finest. That is when he brought you right into the music, right into the heart of his life. Allowing you to enter his space to feel the distress and feel the anguish. This was special space and only in the studio and especially on the stage was he free to allow you in.

He became the master of this type of entertainment and he had his worshippers with him and they loved him. They needed him, but he needed them more.

Slowly he knelt down and began to pick up all the song sheets that had fallen and brought him back into time. He had traveled 75 years back into space in just a few hours.

Frank began to separate the song sheets into their categories. Those for tonight's show, those for *In the Wee Small Hours*, and those special few of Ava's songs. He then arose, walked over to his music bookshelf, and placed them all back on the shelf where they had originally been.

He was very careful to place Ava's songs at the bottom of the pile. He was not sure why they should go on the bottom, but as he placed them there, he seemed to sense that by doing so he could let her go.

Over the years she had left his mind and did not appear as often. She would return and haunt him after speaking to her on the phone or making those short visits that he sometimes did when she was in town or when he traveled to where she lived or was shooting a picture. But those times of seeing her and hearing her voice had become few and far between.

And now she was dead! She was gone from his life. He could no longer hear or see her face to face.

He thought about that for a while as he finished placing all the work sheets back where they belonged. "It's about time to really let her go. I know I tried to do it hundreds of times, but now, I've got to do it. It's really over. Death makes things so final." He spoke this to himself for reassurance not really believing, but he had a need to say the words to himself and attempt to let her go.

He went back to the piano, looked down at the keys, and slowly, without thinking, began to play and sing "When you awake . . ." he stopped awkwardly as a tear ran down his cheek.

"Forget her? How?"

He now looked at his watch as he heard the front door shut and Barbara's voice ring out, "I'm home!"

He quickly brushed away the tear and answered her in a rather husky voice. "Okay, I'm comin' up in a minute."

Frank began to walk around the room haphazardly, looking at pictures and awards, reading some and surveying others. He nodded at some of them, read a few lines from others. *This was some life for a high school dropout,* he thought. *God has been good to me.* He nodded his head in affirmation. He had walked himself into a corner, turned, and began to review the whole room from one side to the other. His head was nodding in approval when he spoke out, "All in all, it's been a good life; a few complaints, but a good life."

"Well, let's get on with tonight. I may have needed to get her out of my system. I did spend that one day mourning her, but I never did go over the impact she had on my life, my singing, my bel canto, as Quinny would say." He whispered this to himself and smiled so as to be able to understand the few hours he had spent with her this afternoon. His mind tried to travel back in time again, but he was too exhausted mentally and gave up after a few seconds.

"It's enough," he said. "Enough!" he reaffirmed himself with more vigor in his voice.

"Let's get dressed!" he spoke as if there were others in the room that had to be dressed with him.

His mind began to leave her as he began to walk over to the door, and as he did so, he returned to the songs for the night's show. *Tonight will be better,* he thought. *Tonight I'm ready!* he reaffirmed himself.

"I needed this afternoon to get some stuff out of my system. I'm ready," he exclaimed aloud while shaking his head in affirmation.

As he reached the door, he stopped and turned and began to look at the whole room again from one end to the other, from top to bottom. This took a few seconds. And as he reached for the doorknob, he smiled in satisfaction over what he had seen. He then opened the door and went out.

He no sooner was on the outside, then he quickly turned around, reentered the room, and exclaimed, "I'm still better than those Spanish bums!"

Frank & Ava–
BOOKS–VHS–CDs

BOOKS

DaGneau, Gilles. *Ava Gardner, Beautiful—Wild—Innocent.* Rome: Gremese, 2003.

Gardner, Ava. *Ava: My Story.* New York: Bantam Books, 1990.

Hamill, Pete. *Why Sinatra Matters.* Boston: Little Brown and Company, 1998.

Havers, Richard. *Sinatra.* London: Dorling Kindersley Limited, 2004.

Irwin, Lew. *Sinatra—A Life Remembered.* Philadelphia: Courage Books, 1997.

Jacobs, George, and William Stadiem. *My Life with Frank Sinatra.* New York: Harper Collins Publishers, Inc., 2003.

Kelley, Kitty. *His Way—The Unauthorized Biography of Frank Sinatra.* New York: Bantam Books, 1987.

Pignone, Charles. *The Sinatra Treasures.* New York: Time Warner Book Group, 2004.

Riddle, Nelson. *Arranged by Nelson Riddle.* New York: Warner, 1985.

Sinatra, Nancy. *Frank Sinatra—An American Legend*. Santa Monica: General Publishing Group, Inc., 1995.

Sinatra, Tina, with Jeff Coplon. *My Father's Daughter*. New York: Berkley Books, 2001.

Strunk, Jr., William, and E. B. White. *The Elements of Style*, Third Edition. New York: Macmillan Publishing Co., Inc., 1979.

Sullivan, Robert. *The Editors of Life. Remembering Sinatra—A Life in Pictures*. New York: Time Inc., 1998.

Turner, John Frayn. *Frank Sinatra*. Dallas: Taylor Trade Publishing, 2004.

Frank Sinatra—Wikipedia, The Free Encyclopedia (article).

VHS

Sinatra—The Music Was Just the Beginning. Burbank: Warner Home Video, 1993.

Frank Sinatra—CBS Interview with Walter Cronkite, 1965(?) CDs, lyrics, and booklets.

Columbia Legacy

> Frank Sinatra Sings His Greatest Hits. Sony Music Entertainment, 1997.
>
> The Voice of Frank Sinatra. Sony Music Entertainment, 2003.

Capital

> Frank Sinatra Swing Easy. Capital Records Inc., 1987.

Frank Sinatra Songs for Swingin' Lovers. Capital Records Inc., 1987–1988.

Frank Sinatra, In the Wee Small Hours. Capital Records, Inc., 1991.

Frank Sinatra Duets. Capital Records Inc., 1993.

Sinatra 80th Live in Concert. Capital Records Inc., 1995.

Frank Sinatra Sings for Only the Lonely. Capital Records Inc., 1998.

Nice 'n' Easy. Capital Records Inc., 1999–2002.

Frank Sinatra Classic Duets. Essex Productions Limited Partnership, 2002.

Reprise

Sinatra at the Sands. Time Warner Company, 1966, Original Release.

My Way, Frank Sinatra. Warner Communications Co., 1969, Original Release.

Frank Sinatra Greatest Love Songs. Warner Music Group, 2002.

CPSIA information can be obtained at www.ICGtesting.com
Printed in the USA
BVOW08s1607070915

416916BV00001B/41/P